Puffin Books

UnCanNy!

Uncanny. You wouldn't think a kid could eat so much.

Guts staggered and tottered. He opened his mouth. The kids in the front row screamed as the putrid waterfall splashed down. All over Rabbit.

It's uncanny . . .

Going inside a dead whale.
Turning into a dung beetle.
Catching someone else's tattoos.
Seeing a flying dog.

And it's uncanny the way Paul Jennings tricks you with every story.

Books by Paul Jennings

PAUL JENNINGS

UnCanNy!

Even more surprising stories

Puffin Books

To Lyndu

PUFFIN BOOKS
Published by the Penguin Group
Penguin Books USA Inc., 375 Hudson Street, New York, New York 10014, U.S.A.
Penguin Books Ltd, 27 Wrights Lane, London W8 5TZ, England
Penguin Books Australia Ltd, Ringwood, Victoria, Australia
Penguin Books Canada Ltd, 10 Alcorn Avenue, Toronto, Ontario, Canada M4V 3B2
Penguin Books (N.Z.) Ltd, 182–190 Wairau Road, Auckland 10, New Zealand

Penguin Books Ltd, Registered Offices: Harmondsworth, Middlesex, England

First published in Australia by Penguin Books Australia Ltd, 1988
First published in the United States of America by Viking,
a division of Penguin Books USA Inc., 1991
Published in Puffin Books, 1993
This edition first published by Penguin Books Australia Ltd, 1994
This edition published in Puffin Books, 1995

1 3 5 7 9 10 8 6 4 2

Copyright © Paul Jennings, 1988

The Library of Congress has cataloged the previous Puffin edition as follows:

Jennings, Paul.
Uncanny!: even more surprising stories / Paul Jennings.
p. cm.
Contents: On the bottom—Trashed—Frozen stiff—UFD—Cracking up—
Greensleeves—Mousechap—Spaghetti pig-out—Know all.
ISBN 0-14-034909=x
1. Children's stories, Australian. 2. Fantastic fiction, Australian.
[1. Supernatural—Fiction. 2. Short stories.] I. Title.
[PZ7.J429874Um 1993] [Fic]—dc20 92-44715 CIP AC

ISBN 0-14-037576-7

Printed in Australia by Australian Print Group
Set in Baskerville

'Trashed' was originally titled 'A Good Trip for Ghosts' in the Australian and British editions
of *Uncanny!*.

CONTENTS

ON THE BOTTOM

1

'It's on the bottom,' says Dad.

'No,' I tell him. 'I've got a fish.'

'It's too big,' says Dad. 'It couldn't be a fish. You're snagged on the bottom.'

He is wrong. I know it is a fish because it is pulling the line out. Snags don't pull on the line.

My rod starts to bend and the line goes whizzing out. Whatever it is I know one thing. I have hooked a whopper.

'You're right, it is a fish,' yells Dad. 'And it's a big one. It's even rocking the boat. Give me the rod, you might lose it.'

Dad always does this. As soon as I hook a fish he wants to pull it in. He thinks that a fourteen-year-old kid can't land his own fish. I shake my head and keep winding on the reel. 'Get the gaff,' I shout. 'I can land it – I know I can.'

For the next hour I play my fish. Sometimes he runs deep and fast and the reel screeches like a cooked cat. Sometimes I get it almost to the edge of our hire boat and then off it goes again. 'I hope it's a snapper,' says Dad. 'Snapper are good eating.'

In the end I win. I get the fish to the edge of the boat and Dad pulls him in with the gaff. I am grinning from ear to ear because I have landed him.

'It's only a shark,' says Dad. 'A small shark. Not much good for eating.' He gives a bit of a grin. 'Well done Lucas. You played him well but you might as well throw him back.'

'No way,' I say. 'You can eat shark. Haven't you ever heard of flake?'

'All right,' says Dad, 'but you have to clean it. You caught it. You clean it.' Dad goes down the steps into the little cabin and leaves me up top to clean my shark. It is about a metre long and it is still kicking around on the deck. I open up a can of Fanta and look at the shark while I am drinking it. After a while the shark stops moving and I know it is dead. I get out my cleaning knife and make a long slit along its belly. I throw the innards and other stuff overboard. Seagulls swoop around fighting for the bits.

Finally I come to the shark's stomach. I decide to look inside and see what it has been eating. This will give me some clues as to what to use for bait. I throw out some fish heads and shells. Then I see something a bit different. I pick up this white, shrivelled thing that looks like a small sausage. For about ten seconds I stare at it. My mind goes numb and I can't quite make sense of what I am seeing. I notice first of all that it has a finger-nail. And a ring. Just below the ring is a small tattoo of a bear. An angry bear.

It is a finger. I have just taken a human finger out of the shark's stomach.

2

I give an almighty scream. A terrible, fearful scream. At the same time I throw my hands up and let go of the finger. It spins in the air like a wheel and then splashes into the sea. Quick as a flash a seagull swoops down and swallows it. The finger has gone.

I have to hand it to that seagull. It swallows the whole finger in one go.

Just then Dad comes rushing up from below. 'What's going on?' he yells. 'Did it bite you?' Dad thinks the dead shark has bitten me.

'No,' I croak. 'A finger. In the shark. A man's finger. With a ring and a bear.'

'What are you babbling about boy?' says Dad. 'What finger?'

'In the shark's stomach. I found a finger. It had a little picture of a bear on it. And a ring. Oooh. Oh. Yuck. It was all shrivelled up and horrible.' As I tell Dad this a little shiver runs down my spine.

Dad goes a bit pale. He has a weak stomach. 'Where is it?' he asks slowly. Dad does not really want to see a human finger but he has to do the right thing and ask to see it.

I point to the empty sky. There is not a seagull in sight. 'A seagull ate it. I dropped it in the sea and a seagull ate it.'

Dad looks at me for a long time without saying anything. Then he starts up the engine. 'We will have to report it to the police. There goes our day's fishing.'

'How did it get there?' I ask slowly.

'Don't ask,' says Dad. 'It's better not to think about it.' Then he stops talking. He is staring at my hand. He is staring so hard at my hand that I think maybe he has never seen a hand before. His face turns red.

He grabs my wrist and starts shaking my arm around. 'What's this?' he yells. 'What on earth have you done?'

'Nothing,' I say. 'I haven't done anything. What are you talking about?' I can tell that Dad is as mad as a snake. Then I look down at my hand and I can see what the matter is. There on the back of my right hand is a little picture. A tattoo of a bear is on the back of one of my fingers.

3

We both gaze at the drawing of the little bear. 'You fool,' yells Dad. 'You've gone and had yourself tattooed. Don't you know that tattoos don't come off? You're stuck with it for life.' He rushes over to the locker and comes back with a whopping big scrubbing brush. He brushes at my hand so hard that my skin goes red. Tears come to my eyes. Dad stops scrubbing and has another look. The little bear is still there. It has a sad expression on its face. I have a sad expression on my face also.

'It came from the finger,' I tell Dad. 'It must have jumped from the finger onto me. The finger from the shark's stomach.'

Dad looks at me through narrowed eyes. 'Don't make it worse boy,' he says angrily. 'Don't add to your folly by making up a pack of lies about a finger. There was no finger.' He shakes his head. 'This is all the thanks I get for everything I've done for you.' He is really angry about the tattoo.

'There was a finger,' I yell. 'There was, there was, there was.'

Dad turns the boat around and heads for the shore. The fishing trip is over. 'Don't you mention one more word about a finger in the shark's stomach,' says Dad. 'You must think that I'm as silly as you. Don't let me hear another word of that cock-and-bull story. Or else.'

It is no good saying anything. He won't listen and I don't really blame him. I can hardly believe it myself. How can a tattoo jump from a dead finger onto a live one? Tattoos don't move. I sit down in the bow and look at my little bear.

This is when I notice something strange. The bear is different. When I first saw my bear he had all four feet on the ground. Now he has one paw pointing. Pointing out to sea. I move my hand around so that the paw is pointing to the shore. The bear turns around. My tattoo moves. It turns around so that its paw once more points out to sea.

The tattoo is alive and it is pointing out to sea.

'It moved,' I say to Dad. He shakes his head. He won't

listen. 'The bear can move,' I yell. 'It is pointing out to sea.' Dad revs up the engine and heads for shore even faster than before.

I look at the bear again. It seems to be staring back at me. It wants something. It wants us to go out to sea.

'Go the other way,' I say to Dad. 'The tattoo wants us to head out to sea.'

Dad turns off the engine and the boat stops. He is staring at me with wild eyes. I can tell that he thinks I have gone crazy. Either that or he thinks I am the biggest liar in the world. 'Come here Lucas,' he says. 'We need to have a talk.' He goes down the steps into the cabin.

Quick as a flash I hop up and slam the cabin door. I slide the bolt across and lock Dad inside. He starts to bang and yell but I don't let him out. Instead I start up the boat and head away from shore. The bear knows best. I decide to follow the bear.

4

I push the throttle forward and the boat surges forward at full speed. The bear is nodding its little head. It thinks I am doing a good job. It is a nice little bear really. I am quite pleased to have it.

'Let me out,' yells Dad.

The bear shakes its head.

'No,' I say.

'Don't go out of sight of land,' shouts Dad. 'We'll get lost.'

'We have the compass,' I say. 'And the bear. The bear

knows where to go.' I am not quite sure but I think I hear a groan come from down in the cabin.

'Look at the petrol,' yells Dad. 'For heavens sake don't use up more than half or we'll never get back.'

He has a point there. I look at the bear on my finger for guidance. It is still waving me on. The sea is becoming rough and the sky is growing dark but on we go. On and on until we can no longer see the land. A wind gets up but still my bear waves me on. The sun is sinking low and clouds are starting to race across the sky. The petrol gauge is showing half full.

And then I see it. A tiny speck on the horizon. 'Is this it?' I say to my tattoo. I am very fond of this little bear. It is nice having a little helper around when you need him.

The bear gives me a paws-up signal. This is it. This is what we have come for.

The speck grows larger and larger until I can see that it is a small rowing boat. There does not seem to be anyone aboard. Dad is still yelling and banging from below but I don't take any notice of him. I slow the boat down and stop next to the dinghy. There is someone in it. A man lying in the bottom. He is lying very still. Very still indeed.

5

I stop the boat and let Dad out. Without a word he rushes over to the edge and looks into the boat. 'See if he's alive,' says Dad. 'I'll get some water.'

I climb down into the little boat and peer at the

unconscious figure. He is dressed only in a pair of faded shorts. One hand is wrapped in a bloodstained handkerchief. I can see at a glance that the man has a finger missing. I can also see something else. He is covered, absolutely covered, in tattoos.

There is not one bit of skin that does not have tattoos on it. There are skulls with toothless smiles. There are tigers and forests. There are daggers with snakes twined around them. There is a large heart with 'Sophie' written in it. There are mermaids and eagles. There is even an eye on the bald patch on his head. The tattooed man is terrific. But is he alive?

I put my hand down to see if he has a pulse. I feel just under his neck like they do in the movies. And then it happens. You may not believe this but it really does happen.

The tattoos start to move. It is sort of like pulling out the plug in a bath and watching the water run out. The tattoos swirl and slide across his skin. They move in a rush. They pour across his flesh to the same spot. His neck. And from his neck they move on – and out. They swarm up my arm and flow across my chest. Before I can blink the whole lot have completely covered me. I am a tattooed boy. And he has clear, white skin. Not one tattoo is left on him. Not one.

I give a shriek and fall over backwards in the dinghy. I am covered in a zoo of animals, birds, plants and people.

Dad climbs down and holds up water to the non-tattooed man's lips. He swallows. He is alive.

The trip back is a nightmare. The man without the

tattoos lies unconscious below. Dad drives the boat flat
out for home. I sit staring in the mirror. My whole face
is covered in tattoos. They are also on my ears, nose,
cheeks and even my eyelids. They cover my chest, my
back, my arms and my legs. I sneak a look inside my
underpants but thank goodness there are none down
there.

We finally get home and the man is taken to
hospital.

So am I.

There is nothing the doctors can do for me. Tattoos
don't come off. No one believes our story about the
shark or the tattoos. The doctors all think Dad and I
are mad or delirious. They are especially angry with
Dad for letting his son get himself tattooed all over his
body. There is talk of taking me away from Dad and
putting me in a home.

The man without the tattoos does not wake up. He
is in a coma.

Finally they let Dad and me go home. I sit in the
house feeling very sorry for myself indeed. I scrub and
scrub but the tattoos are there to stay. The love heart
with 'Sophie' written on it is right in the middle of my
forehead. I know what my girlfriend Cheryl will think
of that. I am too worried to leave the house – I don't
want anyone to see me.

The little bear is still there on my finger although he is
difficult to see among all the tigers and snakes. He seems
to smile at me. I wouldn't mind keeping the bear but I
do not want the rest. These tattoos have ruined my life. I
can't go to school. I won't be able to get a job. I will have

to be a tattooed boy in a circus. Sitting there for everyone to gaze at. How embarrassing. I start to cry. Little tears roll across the mermaids on my cheeks.

6

Weeks pass and I do not leave the house. I sit in my room without talking to anyone. Now and then the little bear seems to wave at me. He is my only friend. I would not like to lose the bear but I would give anything to get rid of the other tattoos.

Then, one day, there is a knock on the door. It is the man without the tattoos. He has recovered from his coma. Dad invites him in and tells him to sit down.

The man thanks us for saving his life. He is grateful that we found him in the dinghy. His boat had drifted out to sea and he would have died if my little bear hadn't showed us where he was. After a bit of this polite chat, Tattooless gets down to the point. 'Look, Lucas,' he says, 'you have some things of mine and I want them back.'

He is talking about the tattoos. It turns out that he is a tattooed man from the sideshows. 'They are the best tattoos in the world,' he says. 'They cost me thousands of dollars. And the pain. Oh the pain. It hurts to get them done. I have sat for hundreds of hours while they drilled away at me. And all for nothing. You've got the lot. The tattoos all nicked off and left me. Except the bear. The shark got that when I put my hand over the side of the boat.'

'But why?' I say. 'Why would they leave?'

'Have you ever thought,' says Tattooless, 'what happens to tattoos when you die? They thought I was done for. They were getting out of it like rats deserting a sinking ship. They didn't want to shrivel up with me when I died so they cleared out onto you. But now I want them back.'

'How?' I ask. A nasty thought comes into my mind. I saw a man skin a rabbit once.

'They might come back to me,' says Tattooless. 'After all, it's a bit crowded on you. You're not as big as me and the tattoos are all bunched up.'

I have to admit that he has a point there.

'Hold out your hand,' he orders. I hold out my hand and we shake like old friends. Nothing happens. We stand there clasping each other for quite a while. Suddenly, with a rush, the tattoos start to move. The whole lot swirl and twirl like slides shining on a moving curtain. They drain off down my arm and back to their owner.

We all grin. I have no tattoos and Tattooless is not tattooless any more. He is covered all over in his drawings again. The tattoos have left me and returned home.

He stands up and heads for the door. 'Wait,' says Dad. 'Don't go yet. I want to make sure there are none left. You might have missed one.' Dad orders me to take off my clothes. I strip down to my underpants and Dad checks me for tattoos. He does not find any.

'Okay.' says Dad to the tattooed man. 'You can go now.'

The tattooed man holds out his hand but I do not want

to shake. Neither does Dad. We decide to give the shaking a miss and make do with a wave.

7

Well that is just about the end of the story. Dad does another check for tattoos but he doesn't find any. I'm glad he doesn't look down the back of my underpants though.

Otherwise he might see my little bear behind.

TRASHED

1

Dad was scabbing around in the rubbish.

'How embarrassing,' said Pete, 'It's lucky there's no one else here to see us.'

I looked around the dump. He was right. No one was dumping rubbish except us. There was just Dad, me, and my twin brother Pete. The man driving the bulldozer didn't count. He was probably used to people coming to the dump with junk and then taking a whole pile of stuff back home.

It was a huge dump with a large, muddy pond in the middle. I noticed a steer's skull on a post in the water. There were flies everywhere, buzzing and crawling over the disgusting piles. Thousands of seagulls were following the bulldozer looking for rotten bits of food.

'These country dumps are fantastic,' yelled Dad. 'Come and help me get this.' He was trying to dig out an old pram. I looked around and groaned. Another car had just pulled up. It was a real flash one. A Mercedes.

We had just arrived in Allansford the day before. It was a little country town where everybody would know what was going on. Pete and I had to start at a new school the next day. The last thing we wanted was someone to see us digging around in the dump.

A man and a boy got out of the Mercedes. They had a neat little bag of rubbish which the man dropped onto the ground. A cloud of flies rose into the air, 'Let's get out of here,' the man said to the boy. 'This place stinks.'

The boy was about my age but he was twice as big as me. He had red hair and he looked tough. I could see that he was grinning his head off and staring at our car. The back seat of our old bomb was full of Dad's findings. There was a mangled typewriter, a baseball bat, two broken chairs, a torn picture of a green lady lying on a tree branch and a bike with no wheels. I blushed. Dad just could not go to the dump without taking half of it back home with him.

I looked up at the kid with red hair again. He was pointing at Dad and laughing fit to bust. 'Oh no,' groaned Pete. 'Look what he has got now.'

Dad had run over to the bulldozer and held up his hand to stop the driver. He was digging around in front of its blade. He had found an arm sticking out of the junk. It looked like a human arm but it wasn't. It was the arm of one of those shop dummies they put dresses on. Dad pulled and yelled and jiggled until he got the whole thing out. Then he stood there holding it up for all the world to see. A female shop dummy with no clothes on.

It had a wig for hair but apart from that it was stark naked. Its left arm pointed up at the sky. It looked like

Dad was standing there with a naked woman. The red-haired kid and his father were both laughing by now. The boy bent down and picked up something from the ground. Then they got into their Mercedes and disappeared through the gate. Pete and I hung our heads with shame. We couldn't bring ourselves to look as Dad dragged the dummy back to the car. I hoped like anything that the red-haired kid didn't go to Allansford School.

'Wonderful,' hooted Dad as he examined the shop dummy. 'Your mother will be pleased. She can use this for making dresses.'

'Don't give me that,' yelled Pete. 'You promised Mum that you wouldn't bring anything back from the dump.'

Dad looked a bit sheepish. 'This is different boys. This isn't junk. This is valuable stuff. Now give me a hand to get this dummy into the car.'

'Not me,' I said.

'Nor me,' added Pete. 'I'm not touching her. She hasn't got any clothes on. It's rude.'

2

There was no room in the back of the car so Dad sat her up in the front. He put the seatbelt on her to stop her falling over. Her lifted-up arm poked through a rust hole in the roof.

'Where are we suposed to sit?' I asked. 'There's no room in the back.'

'One on each side of her,' said Dad. 'We'll all sit in the front. There's plenty of room.'

So that's how we went home. Shame. Oh terrible

shame. Driving along the road with a naked dummy sitting between us. Every time we passed someone Pete and I ducked down so that they couldn't see us. Dad just laughed. It was all right for him. He wasn't starting at a new school in the morning.

Then it happened. A blue flashing light. A siren. A loud voice saying, 'Pull over driver.'

It was the police.

A policeman got off his motorbike and walked slowly to the car. He pulled off his gloves and adjusted his sunglasses. Then he leaned in the window. 'What's this naked lady . . .?' he started off in a cross voice. But then he started laughing. He doubled up holding his side and pointing to the dummy. 'We had a report that there was a naked woman,' he managed to get out in between gasps. 'But it's only a shop dummy.'

I thought he was never going to stop laughing but finally he said, 'Where did you get all this stuff sir?'

'The Allansford dump,' answered Dad.

'The locals call it Haunted Dump,' said the policeman with a grin. He seemed to want to stay and talk. He probably was trying to figure out if Dad was a nut case or not. Pete and I just sat there trying not to be seen. 'No one will go there after dark,' he told us. 'They say the ghost of Old Man Chompers walks that dump at night.'

'Old Man Chompers?' said Dad.

'Yes, he was the caretaker of the dump long ago. They say he was minding his two grandchildren there one day. The children disappeared and were never found. The ground collapsed and all the rubbish fell into a huge hole. People think the children were buried under piles of rubbish. Their bodies were never discovered because the hole filled up with water and formed a lake. Not long after that Old Man Chompers died. People have said that they have seen him walking the dump at night. He pokes at the rubbish, turning things over. He is looking for his lost grandchildren. He moans and groans and calls out for his lost darlings.'

I shivered and looked at Pete. 'You won't catch me going to that dump again,' I said.

'Good,' said the policeman. 'It's a dangerous spot. No place for kids. Anyway – it is said that Old Man Chompers can't leave the dump until he finds his darlings. He has to stay there until he finds them. That's why he wanders the lonely dump at night. He might think that you two would do instead if he caught you there.' Then he said something that made my knees wobble.

'His grandchildren were twins. And Old Man Chompers had poor eyesight. He might mistake you boys for his lost children.' The policeman looked us straight in the eyes and then turned and walked off, chuckling as he went.

3

The next day Pete and I started at Allansford School. It was even worse that we thought it would be. The red-haired kid was waiting at the gate with his tough mates. 'Here they are,' he yelled with glee. 'The twins from the dump.' In a loud voice he started to tell everyone about Dad and the naked shop dummy. Pete and I looked at each other helplessly. We couldn't deny the story. It was true. I could feel tears starting to form behind my eyes. I had to stop them escaping so I blinked real hard. I noticed that Pete was doing the same thing.

It is bad enough starting a new school at the best of times. But when you have to live down something like this it is just terrible. Fortunately the bell went and we had to go inside.

At recess time though, it was even worse. 'I'm the top dog here,' said the red-haired boy. His name was James Gribble. He pushed Pete in the chest. 'What's your name kid?' he asked roughly.

'Pete.'

Gribble gave a twisted grin. 'This twin is Pete, so this one,' he said, pointing at me, 'must be Repeat. Pete and Repeat, the scabby twins from the dump.' All the kids started to laugh. Some of them weren't laughing too loudly though. I could see that they didn't like Gribble much but they were too scared of him to do anything.

After the laugher died down Gribble went and fetched a shoebox with a small hole in the end. 'I'm the boss here,' he said. 'Every new kid has to take my nerve test. If you pass the nerve test you are okay. If you won't do it I thump you every day until you do.' He held up a clenched fist. The kids all crowded around to see what would happen.

The shoebox had a lid which was tied on with string. Gribble pushed the box into my hand. 'Seeing you like the dump so much Repeat,' he leered. 'I have brought something back from there for you. One of you two has to have enough nerve to put your hand in there and take out the mystery object that I found at the dump.'

Pete and I looked at the hole in the box. There was just room enough to put a hand inside.

'Go on,' said Gribble. 'Or you get your first thump now.'

I don't mind telling you that I was scared. There was something in the box from the dump. It could be anything. A dead rat. Or even worse; a live rat. Or maybe a loaded mouse trap. My mind thought of the most terrible things. I didn't want to do it but then I noticed one of the kids was nodding to me. A little kid with a kind face. He seemed to be telling me that it was okay.

I looked at Gribble. I have always heard that you should fight a bully when they first pick on you. Then if you fight hard and hurt them they will leave you alone. Even if you lose the fight everyone will respect you and it will be okay. I sighed. Gribble was twice as big as Pete and me put together. And he had tough mates. They would wipe the floor with both of us. Things like teaching the bully a lesson only happen on TV.

Slowly I pushed my hand into the box. At first I couldn't feel anything but then I touched something hard and slimy. It was sort of horseshoe shaped. I shivered. It was revolting. There were rows of little sharp pointed things. Then I felt another one the same. There were two of them. They reminded me of a broken rabbit trap. They felt like they were made of plastic covered in dry mould. I didn't have the faintest idea what I was holding but all sorts of horrible things came into my mind.

Slowly I pulled out my hand and looked. It was a set of old, broken false teeth.

They were chipped and cracked and stained brown. They felt yucky but I smiled at the circle of kids around me. Pete was grinning too. I had passed the nerve test. Or so I thought.

'Okay Repeat,' said Gribble with a horrible leer. 'You have passed the first bit of the test.' My heart sank. So did Pete's. I didn't realise that there was going to be something else.

Gribble pushed his face up against mine. He had bad breath. 'Now boys,' he growled, 'you have to take the false teeth back where they came from. Back to the dump.' He paused, and then he added, 'At night.'

Pete and I looked at each other. Goose bumps ran up and down our arms. Before we could say anything Gribble told us the next bit. 'And just to make sure that you really go. That you don't just pretend to go. You have to bring something back with you. You have to bring back the steer's skull in the middle of the dump pond. By tomorrow morning. You have to prove that you went to the dump at night by bringing back the skull.'

Pete and I spent the rest of the day worrying. We couldn't concentrate on our school work. I got two out of twenty for my Maths. Pete got four out of twenty. The teacher must have thought that the new kids were real dumb.

That afternoon the boy who had nodded at me in the yard passed me a note. It said:

You had better get the skull. Gribble is real
mean. He punched me up every day for a month
until I passed his rotten nerve test.
Signed, your friend Troy

I passed the note on to Pete. He didn't say anything but he didn't look too good.

After school we walked sadly out of the gate. As we went Gribble yelled at us, 'Have a nice night *my darlings.*'

Neither of us could eat any tea that night. Mum looked at us in a funny way but she didn't say anything. She thought we were just suffering from nerves about the new school. She was right. But only partly. We were also thinking about the ghost of Old Chompers and his lonely search for his lost darlings. I looked at Pete and he looked at me. It was like staring in a mirror. It reminded me that Old Chompers' lost grandchildren were twins too.

'We could pretend to be sick tomorrow,' I said to Pete after tea.

'It wouldn't work,' he answered. 'Mum never gets fooled by that one. Anyway, we would have to go back to school sooner or later.'

'We could tell Dad and . . .'

'Oh sure,' put in Pete before I could finish. 'And he will tell the teachers and everyone in the school will call us narcs.'

'What about throwing the false teeth in the bin and getting a steer's skull from somewhere else?' I yelled. 'Gribble would never know that we hadn't really been to the dump.'

Pete looked at me as if I was a bit crazy. 'Great,' he answered in a cross voice. 'And where are you going to get a steer's skull at this time of night? It can't be any old steer's skull you know. It has to have white horns and horrible teeth. No – we will have to do it. We will take the false teeth back to the dump and bring the steer's skull back with us. There's nothing to be scared of really. Ghosts

21

aren't true. There aren't any ghosts. People just think they see them when they are scared.

I nodded my head without saying anything. I was scared already. And I didn't even want to *think* that I saw a ghost. But I knew Pete was right. We would have to go. It was the only way.

4

That night after Mum and Dad had gone to bed we snuck out of the window and headed off for the dump. We walked slowly along the dusty road which wound through the moonlit paddocks. Pete carried a rope with a hook on the end for getting the skull out of the middle of the pond. I carried a torch in one hand and the false teeth in the other. They felt all slimy and horrible. I sure was looking forward to getting rid of them.

There was not a soul to be seen. The crickets were chirping their heads off and now and then an owl would hoot. Cows sat silently in the dry grass on the other side of the barbed-wire fences. I was really scared but for some reason the cows made me feel a little better. I don't know why this was because if anything happened the cows weren't going to help. Basically a cow is just a cow.

The further we got from home the more my knees started to wobble. I kept thinking that every shadow hid something evil and terrible. The inside of my stomach wall felt like a frog was scribbling on it with four pencils.

Our first problem started when we reached the dump. It had a high wire fence around it with barbed wire on the top. And the gates were locked. A gentle wind was blowing and the papers stuck to the fence flapped and sighed.

'How are we going to get in?' I asked Pete. Secretly I was hoping we would have to go home.

'Climb over,' he said.

We threw over the rope with the hook on it and clambered up the high wire fence. The wire was saggy and it started to sway from side to side with our weight. We ended up perched on the top trying to get our legs over the barbed wire. Suddenly the whole fence lurched over and sent us crashing onto the ground on the inside. Then the fence sprang back up again with the rope on the other side.

'Ouch, ow, ooh . . . that hurt,' I yelled. I rubbed my aching head.

'Quiet,' whispered Pete fiercely. 'You're making enough noise to wake the dead.'

His words sent a chill up my spine. 'I wish you hadn't said that,' I whispered back.

Pete looked up at the fence. We were trapped inside. 'We will never get back over that,' he said. I could tell that he was thinking the same thing as me. What fools we were. What were we doing in a lonely dump in the middle of the night? There was no one to help us. There was not another soul there. Or was there?

A little way off, behind some old rusting car bodies, I thought I heard a noise. Pete was looking in the same direction. I was too terrified to move. I wanted to run but my legs just wouldn't work. I opened my mouth to scream but nothing came out. Pete stood staring as if he was bolted to the ground.

It was a rustling, tapping noise. It sounded like someone digging around in the junk, turning things over. It was coming in our direction. I just stood there pretending to be a dead tree or a post. I wished the moon would go in and stop shining on my white face. The tapping grew louder. It was coming closer.

And then we saw it. Or him. Or whatever it was. An old man, with a battered hat. He was poking the ground with a bent stick. He was rustling in the rubbish. He came on slowly. He was limping. He was bent and seemed to be holding his old, dirty trousers up with one hand. He came towards us. With a terrible shuffle.

Pete and I both noticed it at the same time. His feet weren't touching the ground. He was moving across the rubbish about thirty centimetres above the surface.

It was the ghost of Old Man Chompers.

We both screeched the same word at exactly the same moment. 'Run.'

And did we run. We tore through the waist-high rubbish. Scrambling. Screaming. Scrabbling. Not noticing the waves of silent rats slithering out of our way. Not feeling the scratches of dumped junk. Not daring to turn and snatch a stare at the horrible spectre who hobbled behind us.

Finally, with bursting lungs, we crawled into the back of an old car. It had no doors or windows so we crouched low, not breathing, not looking, not even hoping.

Why had we come to this awful place? Fools, fools, fools. Suddenly the thought of Gribble and the steer's skull and the false teeth seemed stupid. I would have fought a thousand Gribbles rather than be here. Trapped in a dump with a ghost.

I could feel Pete trembling beside me. And I could hear the voice of someone else. A creaking, croaking cry. 'My darlings . . . my darlings . . . my darlings . . my darlings.'

5

I knew it. I just knew it. The ghost of Old Man Chompers had seen us. He thought we were his lost darlings. His dead grandchildren. He was coming to get us. Then he would be able to leave this place. And take us with him. To that great ghost dump in the sky.

I thought of Mum and Dad. I thought of my nice warm bed. I would never see them again. Our parents would never know what had happened to us. Never know that we had come to our end in the bowels of the Allansford Dump.

'At last, at last . . . my darlings . . . at last.' The wailing voice was nearby. He knew where we were. Without a word we bolted out of the car. We fled blindly across the festering dump until we reached the pond. The deep black pond, filled with floating foulness.

And behind, slowly hobbling above the bile, came the searching figure of Old Chompers. We were trapped against the edge of the pond.

In panic we looked around for escape. Mountains of junk loomed over us on either side. To the back was the pond and to the front . . . we dared not look.

'Quick,' yelled Pete. 'Help me with this.' He was pulling at an old rusty bath. Dragging it towards the water.

'It won't float,' I gasped. 'Look at the plughole. The water will get in. It'll sink.'

Pete bent down and scratched up a dollop of wet clay from the edge of the water. He jammed it into the plughole. 'Come on,' he panted. 'Hurry.'

The bath was heavy but terror made us strong. We launched it out into the murky water. Then we scrambled in. Just in time. The bath rocked dangerously from side to side but slowly it floated away from the approaching horror.

We paddled frantically with our hands until the bath reached the middle of the pond. Then we stopped and stared at Old Chompers. He hobbled to the edge of the water. He staggered towards us. He was walking on the water. His hands outstretched. 'My darlings,' he groaned. 'My long lost darlings.' Pete and I clung to the sides of the bath with frozen fingers.

The moon went in and everything was black.

Suddenly there was a pop. The clay plug shot into the air followed by a spout of water. Brown wetness swirled in the bath. We were sinking. In a flash we found ourselves swimming in the filthy water. We both headed for the shore, splashing and shouting and struggling. Pete was a better swimmer than me. He disappeared into the gloom.

My jumper soaked up water and dragged me down. I went under. I came up again and spat out the lumpy brown liquid. I knew I would drown unless I could find something to grab on to. The bath was gone.

Then my hand touched something. It was a post with something on the end. I grabbed onto it and kicked towards the shore. As my feet touched the bottom I realised that the post had horns. Then I saw that it had a face. A staring dead face with sharp teeth. It was the horrible leering steer's skull.

I screamed and crawled over to where Pete lay on the shore.

We were both soaked to the skin. We were cold and exhausted. We were too tired to move.

The ghost of Old Man Chompers crept across the water with outstretched hands. His face was wrinkled like a bowl of hard, cold custard. His mouth was as a black hole formed in the custard by a vanished golf ball. He chuckled as he looked at me.

In my left hand I still had the false teeth. All the time I had been running I had held onto them. I had no other weapon so I held them out in front of me. My fingers were shaking so much that it made them chatter.

As the ghost of Old Man Chompers jumped at me I screamed and screamed and tried to push him off with the teeth.

He grabbed the false teeth from my quivering fingers and shoved them into his mouth. 'At last,' he said. 'I've found them. My darlings. My darlings.' He opened and closed his mouth with joy, making sucking noises as he did it.

After a bit of this he pulled out a ghostly apple from his pocket and started to chomp on it. 'Wonderful,' he cackled. 'Wonderful. You don't know what it was like without my darlings . . . I owe you boys a big favour for bringing these back.'

We both lay there looking at the grinning ghost. Suddenly he didn't seem so scary. Pete found his voice first. 'You mean,' he said. 'That your darlings are your false teeth? Not your long-lost grandchildren?'

The ghost started to cackle even more. 'Them,' he said. 'Them brats. What would I want them for? I told 'em not to play around here. Told 'em it was dangerous. No I was lookin' for these.' He smacked his lips again and showed the cracked, brown teeth. 'Couldn't leave without these. Been lookin' for 'em for years. Now I can go. Now I can leave this rotten dump and join all the others.' As he said this he started to fade away. I knew that we would never see him again.

'Wait,' yelled Pete. 'Don't go. Come back.'

Chompers stopped fading and looked at Pete. 'What?' he said. 'What do yer want?' I could see that he was in a hurry. He didn't want to hang around the dump for any longer than he had to.

Pete looked the ghost straight in the eye. 'You said that you owe us a big favour for bringing your teeth back. Well we want to be paid back. We want one favour before you go.'

'Well,' said Old Chompers with a chipped smile. 'What is it?'

6

Old Chompers wasn't the only one who didn't want to hang around that dump. He showed us a hole in the fence and we ran back down that road as fast as we could go.

When we got back to Allansford we climbed up a certain tree and looked in a certain window.

Gribble was fast asleep in bed. He had a big smile on his face. He had fallen asleep thinking about how smart he was making those dumb twins go to the dump in the middle of the night.

Suddenly he was awakened by a noise. It sounded like a person tapping with a stick. It was coming towards his window. Then he heard a croaky voice. 'My darling,' it said. 'At last I've found my darling.'

Gribble was terrified. He wanted to scream but nothing would come out.

A terrible figure floated through the wall. He had a face which was wrinkled like a bowl of hard, cold custard. His mouth was as a black hole formed in the custard by a vanished golf ball. And in that black hole was a pair of cracked old false teeth.

The ghost chuckled as he held the horrible skull over Gribble's head. 'I think you wanted this,' he said as he dropped his load on Gribble's face.

'That was from Pete,' he screeched. 'And this,' he yelled picking it up again, 'is a Repeat.'

Gribble didn't feel the steer's skull the second time. Nor did he see the ghost fade away. He had fainted.

The next day at school though, James Gribble was very nice to me and Pete. I had never met a more polite boy. And there is one thing I can tell you for a fact – he never mentioned anything about being the top dog ever again.

FROZEN STIFF

'Where will I put it?' asked Old Jack Thaw in a creaky voice.

I looked at the mouse. Its frozen tail stuck out straight behind it like an arrow. It was poised with one frozen leg raised as if it was sniffing the air. Its frozen eyes stared ahead without blinking

Jack Thaw had never been to school and he couldn't read or write too well. That's why he needed me. I always stopped off at Jack's place on the way home from school.

'Well,' I said, 'mouse starts with 'M'. That comes between 'L' and 'N'. So you have the lizard on one side and the numbat on the other.' I pointed at a space between the little ice blocks.

Jack Thaw gave a wrinkly grin. His bare gums showed because he had forgotten to put in his false teeth. He picked up the lizard's ice block and moved it a little bit to the left. Then he placed the frozen mouse in its place on the shelf. It seemed to glare at us from inside its icy prison.

We both stood and stared at the collection of tiny animals. Birds, spiders. Bats, rats. Grasshoppers, goannas. Fleas, flies. You name it, if it was small and dead it was there. The walls of the freezing room were lined with shelves. On the shelves were thousands of small ice blocks – each one with a tiny creature frozen inside.

Long ago, this had been an ice factory. And Jack Thaw had been an ice man. He used to take blocks of ice around to people's houses on the back of an old truck. But gradually people stopped needing the ice. They sold their ice chests and bought fridges instead. In the end no one wanted ice at all.

So Jack stopped working and started up his collection. Whenever he found a small, dead creature he brought it back to the ice works and froze it inside an ice block. Then he put it on a shelf inside his huge freezer room. This room was so big that you could drive a truck inside it if you wanted to.

A shiver ran up my spine. 'Let's go outside,' I said. 'I'm cold.'

We walked out of the freezer room into the factory. Jack swung the massive doors closed. Then he pointed to the bandage on my finger. 'Have you hurt yourself?' he asked.

I nodded and took off the stained bandage. My finger was bleeding from a deep cut. 'Barbed-wire,' I said. 'I cut it on the barbed-wire on Gravel's fence.'

Jack took me over to a huge steel bin on wheels. It was

full of salty water. Jack would never usually let me near this bin of water. It was special. He used tap water to freeze the animals. Once I had seen Jack drink a bit of the salty water when he didn't know I was there.

Jack climbed up the side of the bin and dipped in a glass. He held the glass out to me. 'Put your finger in there,' he said.

Without a word I dipped in my bleeding finger.

When I pulled it out my finger had stopped bleeding.

Jack smiled, 'Wonderful stuff, salt water,' he said. Then he shook a gnarled old hand at me. 'Don't you tell anyone about this,' he croaked. 'Or my collection.'

'Don't worry,' I said with a sigh. 'I've told you a million times. I can keep a secret. No one knows about your frozen zoo. Not even Mum.'

Some of the kids at school said that Jack was 200 years old. They were scared of him. I was the only person he ever let in the ice factory.

I walked towards the outside door.

'Come back tomorrow,' said Jack. 'I'm going to the beach. I might find a dead fish. You will have to show me where to put it.' He sure was a funny bloke. All he ever thought about was his precious collection. But he had a heart of gold. He was a good mate.

I waved goodbye. 'See you,' I said. 'I'd better be going. I haven't said goodbye to Jingle Bells yet. I rushed off without saying goodbye to her when I cut my finger.'

2

Jingle Bells was a cow. You might wonder what a cow

was doing in the middle of the city. Well, it was the saddest thing. Poor old Jingle Bells was locked in a shed. In the shadow of the high-rise flats. In between the factories and the freeways. Stuck in the polluted, smelly city. Surrounded by smog. Like us.

Only it was worse for a cow.

Jingle Bells had never grazed in the grass. Never stepped on a flower. Never snatched a glimpse of the sky. She was a prisoner in Gravel's shed. He sure was a mean bloke.

Every day for the last two weeks she had been mooing. Long sad moos. They went on and on without stopping.

Jack had told me it was because it was Springtime. 'It's the smell of the country,' he had said. 'In between the fumes and the foul air, a tiny bit of pollen from the country is carried on the wind. It gets through a crack in the dark shed. It creeps across the concrete floor. It snakes into Jingle Bells' nostrils. And then she smells the pollen – the little messenger from the bush. It tells her that far away there are other cows. It speaks of soft winds – and blossoms that bend the branches of trees until they touch the cool clover. She moos for the moon and the stars and the dew of the still, cold nights.'

Jack Thaw might not be able to read. But he sure had a way with words. Every time I thought of Jingle Bells after that a tear would come into my eye.

Something had to be done. It was wrong to keep a cow locked up in a dingy shed.

Jingle Bells was my best friend after Jack Thaw. Not that she had ever seen me. She had only heard my voice. And looked into my eye.

Every night after school I would creep along the alley

behind Gravel's house and climb over his back fence. Then I would sneak up to his cow shed and peep through a crack in the palings. Jingle Bells would stare at me through the crack and I would stare back at her. We would stand there for ages – eye to eye. Not moving. Just looking.

You can tell a lot from staring at a cow's eye. I could tell that Jingle Bells wanted to get out. Wanted to escape. I knew that she longed for the sunshine. I knew that she hated Gravel who kept her in this black hole.

Before I left her each night I would poke a little bit of fresh grass through the crack. All Gravel ever gave her was dry old chaff and hay. When Jingle Bells saw the grass she would give six, short, happy moos. They sounded a bit like the first bars of the song 'Jingle Bells'. That's why I named her after the Christmas carol.

Gravel just called her 'the cow'. Whenever he was around, Jingle Bells' long, sad moos could be heard filtering through the sounds of car horns and screeching brakes.

3

Anyway, on the day that it all started I saw something especially sad. I looked through the crack and saw Jingle Bells straining at her rope. She was pulling and pulling. Trying to reach a tiny little patch of sunshine that had leaked in through a hole in the roof. It was only about the size of a twenty-cent coin but Jingle Bells wanted to stand in it. Imagine that. The poor thing wanted to stand in a tiny little splot of sunshine.

I put back my head and gave a scream of rage. Then I turned and ran. I clambered over Gravel's back fence. I sped down the alley. I tore across the road to the high-rise flats where we lived. My lungs felt like fire but nothing could stop me.

The lift seemed to take ages but at last I reached the fifteenth floor. Our flat was number twenty. I banged on the door until Mum finally opened it. 'What's the rush?' she asked.

'The hammer,' I panted. 'Where's the hammer?'

'Under the sink,' answered Mum.

Without another word I went into the kitchen and grabbed our claw-hammer. 'Be back soon,' I yelled. I headed back towards the cow shed as fast as I could go.

There was no sign of Gravel back at the shed. Inside, Jingle Bells was still mooing with long, sad moos and straining to reach the little shaft of sunshine. 'Don't worry old girl,' I said. 'You're in for a big treat.'

I clambered up onto the top of the shed and started pulling out nails with the claw-hammer. It was hard work but after about half an hour I had most of the nails out of one sheet of roofing iron.

There was still no sign of Gravel.

At last it was done. I had freed one large sheet of corrugated iron. I ripped it off the roof and threw it into the small garden. Sunshine poured into the shed. Buckets of it. Bathloads of it. A huge waterfall of light. Pouring, streaming, warming. Flooding down into the shed. It smothered Jingle Bells in its glorious flow. She raised her head and gave six, short happy moos. And then another six, and another and another. For the first time in her life she felt the life-giving gift of a warm sun.

I lay there on the roof for maybe an hour. Maybe two. I couldn't say how long for sure. I gazed down at Jingle Bells as she sunned herself. She settled onto the floor in the sun, chewing her cud. She was probably pretending that she was grazing in a grassy glen. I could see that she was happy.

And then, just as Jingle Bells' patch of sunlight started to climb the walls, I felt an iron grip on my ankle. I felt myself being yanked backwards. My stomach scratched on the hot roof. My nose bumped along the corrugations. 'Help.' I screamed. 'Stop. Stop.' Someone was pulling me off the roof from below. I tried to hang on with my fingers but there was nothing to grab onto.

Suddenly I found myself in mid air. I seemed to hang there for a second or two and then I plunged downwards. I crashed painfully onto the gravel beneath. The wind was knocked from my lungs and I couldn't breathe.

But I could see. And I didn't like what I saw. Gravel was staring down at me with a wild look on his face. His big red nose was lumpy. His false teeth seemed to have a life of their own. They clacked and jumped out of time as he shouted at me. 'You vandal. You, you, brat. What do you mean by wrecking my shed?'

'It's Jingle Bells,' I managed to gasp. 'I'm letting in the sun.'

He just stood there for a second or two with his mouth opening and closing like a goldfish. 'You've pulled the roof off my shed for a cow? For a rotten old cow that doesn't even give any milk?'

'It's cruel,' I yelled. 'It's cruel keeping Jingle Bells in the dark.'

'I'll show you what's cruel,' he shrieked. He picked up a piece of old rope and started lashing at my legs with it. I wriggled out of his way and climbed up over the fence before he could grab me again. I started to run down the lane. Behind me I heard Gravel's last mean words. 'The cow won't want sunshine for much longer. Tomorrow it goes to the knackery.' His voice was raised in a high-pitched laugh.

4

The knackery. The glue factory. He was going to have Jingle Bells killed. And all because of me. It was my fault. I started to cry as I walked home. Salty tears trickled down my face and into my mouth.

I had to save Jingle Bells.

That evening I made my plans. I looked out of my bedroom window at the night lights of the city. The oil refinery was lit up like fairyland. Closer to us I could see the West Gate Bridge arching over the Yarra River. The gate to freedom. The road to the country.

I set my clock radio for midnight. That would give me plenty of time to get Jingle Bells through the city and over the West Gate Bridge. We could get away from the main roads before the traffic started.

I reached out to switch off the light. That's when I noticed that my cut finger was better. There was no sign of the cut at all. It was completely healed.

I was soon asleep. Tossing and turning. And dreaming of a ghostly cow calling, calling, calling to me through the fog.

That night there was a power failure. While I was asleep the lights of the city went out. And my clock radio went off.

Mum woke me at the usual time – seven-thirty. 'Come on,' she said, 'you'll be late for school.'

I looked at the window. Sun was pouring in. 'Oh no,' I yelled. 'The knackery truck might already be on the way.'

'What are you going on about?' said Mum.

'Nothing,' I said. 'Nothing. I don't want any breakfast.' I put on my clothes and rushed off without even saying goodbye.

I crept round the back of Gravel's place. I hoped he was still in bed.

The shed door was locked but I was in luck. My claw-hammer was still lying where it had fallen the day before. I smashed off the lock and went into the gloom. Jingle Bells gave six happy little moos when she saw me.

'Shhh,' I whispered, holding my finger up to my lips. Jingle Bells didn't understand. She was glad to see me and she kept mooing.

'Quiet,' I gasped. 'Gravel will hear you. You don't want to end up in the glue factory do you?' I took the rope that was around Jingle Bells' neck and led her out into the back yard. The only way out was up a path at the side of the house. It led to the front garden and the road. We walked in silence along the path. Just as we reached a low window Jingle Bells let out an enormous bellow. A monstrous, mind-numbing moo.

5

There was no use in being quiet any more. 'Run,' I yelled.

But Jingle Bells didn't want to move. She was blinking in the sunlight. She hadn't been outside before. She was looking at the street and the cars. Then she saw something that did make her run. It was Gravel's bloated, blotchy face. It was like the face of the Devil. Jingle Bells took one look at him and started to run out of the gate and down the road. She was really scared. Her udder swung from side to side as she went. It looked like a swollen rubber glove filled with water.

Cows can run fast when they want to. Jingle Bells was disappearing down the road. Out of the corner of my eye I saw Gravel heading for his car.

Jingle Bells reached a T-intersection. 'Turn right,' I shouted. 'Head for the West Gate Bridge.' Jingle Bells turned left and headed down the main road towards the city. I tried to catch her but she was too fast. She lurched down the road and past Jack Thaw's old ice works. Jack was standing outside hosing down the footpath.

'Help,' I yelled to Jack. 'Get your truck.' Jack looked startled but he disappeared inside the factory as quick as he could go. Jingle Bells kept jogging along with her neck rope trailing behind her. She was heading straight for the centre of the city. I just couldn't catch up.

The frightened cow was running down the middle of Flinders Street. Cars and trucks swerved out of her way. Drivers blasted their horns and yelled out. The footpaths were crowded with people making their way to work. They all stopped and stared at the cow running down the middle of town.

At last Jingle Bells reached the middle of the city. She turned and looked at Flinders Street Station. 'Oh no,' I groaned. 'Don't go up the steps.' But she did. She started to walk up the steps into the station. Waves of people burst out of the gates. A couple of trains must have just arrived. Poor old Jingle Bells just stood there on the steps mooing as the crowd swept past like a mob of sheep dividing around a car on a country road.

I battled through the throng and grabbed her rope. I noticed a policeman coming towards us. He was yelling something about cows on the footpath. I knew that if he caught us he would take my name and address. Then Jingle Bells would be taken back to her owner. And the glue factory.

I looked around for escape. There was only one way to go. 'Come on,' I said. 'Into the station.'

I pulled Jingle Bells up the steps and through one of the ticket gates. The ticket collector jumped up and started yelling. 'Hey,' he shouted. 'Come back here. Where is that cow's ticket?'

We kept running. I turned down a ramp and pulled Jingle Bells through the crowds and onto a platform. A train was about to leave. 'On here,' I said. Jingle Bells followed me onto the train.

The train was packed with people on their way to work. Travellers dressed for work in their best clothes stood or sat in the carriage. Everyone moved over for me and Jingle Bells. Most of the people sitting down just kept reading their papers. The ones standing up just stood there trying not to look at each other the way people do in trains. No one seemed worried that there was a cow in the train.

The train pulled out of the station.

There was a kid in school uniform sitting down in the corner. The bloke next to him suddenly poked this boy in the ribs and pointed at Jingle Bells' udder. 'Can't you see there is a lady standing,' he said. 'Get up and give her your seat.'

Everyone cracked up. The whole carriage burst out laughing. Except me. I was embarrassed. I went red in the face.

'Well I think it is disgusting,' said a woman wearing a white dress. 'You can't bring a cow in here. Not in a first-class carriage.' She was standing right behind Jingle Bells. She poked the poor cow in the side with a sharp umbrella. Jingle Bells only did what any cow does when it is frightened. She lifted up her tail and released a large squirt of cow dung. It splurted out all over the woman's white dress. The woman started screaming and shouting and jumping up and down like nothing.

The train was slowing down. It was Spencer Street Station. Not too far from the West Gate Bridge. 'Come on,' I said to Jingle Bells. 'This is where we get off.'

The people on the platform were so surprised to see a cow in the station that they didn't do a thing. We just sailed out onto the road with no trouble at all.

6

I took Jingle Bells' rope and led her along the freeway.
We kept to the side of the road – out of the way of the
semi-trailers and trucks that roared past. After ages and
ages I caught a glimpse of the West Gate Bridge ahead. It
towered up over the factories high into the sky.

The road started to slope upwards. We were on the
approaches to the bridge. After a while we came to a
large, green sign. It said:

NO BICYCLES OR HORSES ON THE BRIDGE

'It's okay,' I said to Jingle Bells. 'You're not a horse.
And you sure aren't a bike.'

By now the sun was getting up and it was hot. We
started to move up the bridge – higher and higher.
Trucks and cars sounded their horns. Drivers waved at
us. No one had ever seen a boy and a cow crossing over
West Gate before. There was no footpath so we had to
walk in the breakdown lane.

Sweat was starting to form around Jingle Bells' neck.
Every now and then when a very large truck roared by
she would give a nervous shudder. She was scared of the
traffic. She wanted green fields and so far she had only
found black bitumen. 'Don't worry old girl,' I said. 'It
gets better on the other side. Only another couple of
hours and we will start to see the paddocks.' I sounded
cheerful but I was worried. Cows weren't meant to go on
long journeys along hard roads. And Jingle Bells had
never walked anywhere before. What if she conked out?
What if she bolted and I lost her?

I pulled Jingle Bells up to a stop so that we could rest for a while. That's when I saw something good. My heart gave a little extra beat. A long way off behind us, stopped at a red light, was a truck with a little crane on the back.

It was Jack Thaw.

And then I saw something sad.

Gravel in his Volvo. He drove straight through the red light. He was still a long way off but he was coming after us.

'It's Gravel,' I gasped. Jingle Bells understood. Don't ask me how but she did.

She gave one frightened bellow and started to run. I knew that I wouldn't be able to keep up. I would lose her. That's when I did it. That's when I jumped up onto her back.

Jingle Bells trotted along the side of the bridge with me riding on top. I hung on to her horns like grim death. The air was filled with tooting and shouting. The traffic slowed. Everyone wanted to watch the cowboy.

Boy, was I scared. We were right next to the railings on the edge of the bridge. People on the boats beneath looked like tiny insects. In the distance I could see an ocean liner heading along the river towards the sea. We were a long way up. Or I should say, the river was a long way down.

Riding a cow isn't easy. I jolted up and down. I slipped from side to side. My behind was sore from banging on Jingle Bells' bones. At any moment I knew I would fall off. On and on ran Jingle Bells. Up towards the very highest part of the bridge. I couldn't look behind us but I knew that Gravel was not far away.

Suddenly a car swerved in front of us and squealed to a stop. It was Gravel. He had cut us off. Jingle Bells put on the brakes. She skidded to a stop and I went flying over her head. I landed on the bitumen road. I grazed my hands and face. My head hurt like crazy.

'Got you,' screamed Gravel. He was so mad that he was dribbling with anger. 'That cow goes to the glue factory,' he managed to get out. 'And you go to the police station.'

7

Jingle Bells looked at me with her soft, brown eyes. She wanted me to help. But she knew, deep in her heart, that there was nothing I could do. I was only a boy. The poor cow gave one long moo and then jumped up at the railings of the bridge. She was trying to jump off. She managed to get her two front feet over the railings. Then she started pushing forwards with her back legs. She started to topple.

'No,' I shrieked. 'No, no, no.' I grabbed her tail and tried to pull her back. She was too heavy. I couldn't hold her. She was slipping. I clung onto her tail. I couldn't let her go. Over she went. Over the rail and into the air. Tumbling, turning, twisting. Down, down, down.

And with her, still hanging onto the tail, was me.

As we plummeted towards the brown water far below I thought I heard an evil voice from above raised in a cackling laugh.

We seemed airborne for ever. A cow with a boy gripping its tail. Spinning through the smoggy air. I was terrified. And yet in another way I found it peaceful. I saw a snatch of sky. A glimpse of brown river. A toss of tumbling cow. Floating. Falling. Fearing. Like two feathers frozen in time. Down we plunged. Down, down, down.

Crack.

We hit the water. It was the loudest, hardest, bang I have ever known. The river was like concrete. It flattened my bones. Squashed my flesh. Blackened my brain.

For a brief second I felt myself gurgling deep in the water. And then nothing. I must have been knocked out.

The next thing I remember is being dragged along through the river. My hand was still gripping Jingle Bells' tail. She was swimming weakly for the shore. Sometimes my head was above water and sometimes it was under. I had water in my lungs. I coughed and spluttered. I was too tired to swim. All I could do was grip the tail in my tortured fingers.

Jingle Bells saved my life. I would have drowned but for her. She was very weak. Dozens of times her head went under the surface but each time she found new strength. Finally she reached the shore. She staggered up the muddy bank a few steps, dragging me behind her. She turned around and looked at me for a few seconds with those brown eyes. Then she collapsed.

She was dead.

'Jingle Bells,' I sobbed. 'Jingle Bells. Don't leave me.' Her eyes stared forward without blinking. My eyes brimmed with tears.

Now she would never see the green fields and taste the

cool grass. After all this. After everything that had happened. I crawled over to her and twisted up her head. I didn't know what to do. I remembered my first aid. I put my mouth down onto hers and blew. Mouth-to-mouth resuscitation.

But it didn't work. She was too big. Air leaked out over the sides of her frothy tongue and out through her milky teeth. I just didn't have enough puff to fill the lungs of a cow.

I heard the sound of a car door. It was Jack Thaw. He looked at Jingle Bells' still body and ran back to his truck. He ripped off the outside mirror from the truck door. Then he held it in front of Jingle Bells' immobile mouth. 'What are you doing?' I sobbed.

'Looking for fog,' he said. 'If the mirror fogs up it means she is breathing. If there is no fog she is dead.'

We both looked at the mirror. There was no fog.

'Come on,' said Jack. 'There is nothing we can do here.'

'What about Jingle Bells?' I shouted. 'What about Jingle Bells?'

'She will wash out with the tide,' said Jack. 'Out to the bay. It will be a sort of burial at sea.'

'No,' I shouted. The tears were still running down my face. 'I'm not letting the sharks get her. Or the crabs. We are taking her with us.'

'How?' said Jack.

I pointed to the crane on the back of Jack's truck. 'Put some ropes around her and lift her on to the truck.'

'And then where?' asked Jack.

'Back to your place.'

So that is what we did. We gently lowered Jingle Bells onto the back of Jack's truck and took her body to the ice factory.

8

When we got there I went straight over to the big steel bin that Jack kept his freezing water in. It was on wheels. I tried to push it but it was too heavy. I climbed up on the little ladder and looked inside. It was full to the top.

'What are you doing?' said Jack.

'Lower Jingle Bells in,' I said. 'We are going to freeze her. We are going to add her to the collection.'

Jack looked at me for a long time with a funny expression on his face. 'All right,' he said. 'But there is no one else in the world that I would do this for.'

He started up the crane and lowered Jingle Bells' body into the huge bin of water.

'Now,' I told him, 'push the bin into the freezer. Push it in with the truck.' I opened the freezer doors and Jack nudged the steel bin into the freezer. He left the rope hanging out of the bin.

'To get the ice block out with,' said Jack.

We shut the freezer doors. 'How long?' I asked. 'How long till she's frozen?'

'Tomorrow lunch time. By lunch time tomorrow Jingle Bells will be frozen inside the biggest man-made ice block in the world.' We grinned at each other. It was better than letting her wash out to sea.

Just then we heard a loud banging coming from the

street. Jack went over and opened the door to the street. It was Gravel. He was still as mad as a snake. 'Where's my cow?' he yelled. 'I want my cow.'

'It's dead,' said Jack angrily. 'Are you satisfied now?'

Gravel narrowed his eyes. 'A dead cow's worth eighty dollars for pet food,' he said. 'I want it back.'

Jack opened and closed his fist. For a moment I thought he was going to punch Gravel but he didn't. He slammed the door closed in his face. 'Buzz off,' he shouted. 'Jingle Bells stays here.'

Gravel screamed at us through the door. 'I'll be back. Just you see. I'll be back.'

'Ratbag,' said Jack under his breath.

I went home for the night. But Jack slept at the ice works just in case Gravel came back.

At lunch time the next day we opened the freezer. Jack backed in the crane and attached it to the rope. The crane groaned and smoked. Nothing happened. It had never lifted anything so heavy before. 'Try again,' I yelled.

This time the ice block started to move. Slowly at first – and then with a 'pop' and a 'slurp' it jumped out of the bin. Jack lowered it to the floor.

And there stood Jingle Bells. Inside the great block of ice. A frozen statue. Her unblinking eyes seemed to stare at us. But I knew they couldn't see anything.

'Where does she go?' asked Jack.

'Well,' I said, 'Jingle Bells starts with 'J'. 'J' comes between 'I' and 'K'. You will have to put her between the ibis and the kookaburra.' Jack started up the truck and pushed Jingle Bells' icy home against the wall in front of the kookaburra. Then he started filling the bin up again with tap water.

'Leave the hose running on its own,' I said to Jack. 'I want to talk to you.'

We went outside and shut the freezer door. 'Look,' I said, 'it's not right to leave poor old Jingle Bells there. She is still locked inside. There are no windows in the freezer. It's just like in the shed. I want her to be under the blue sky. In a paddock of grass. And anyway, Gravel might come back and get her. We have to take Jingle Bells to the country.'

Jack scratched his head. 'You're right,' he said. Let's do it now.'

9

We loaded Jingle Bells' ice block onto the back of the truck and drove off. We didn't care what people thought. We drove out over the West Gate Bridge with Jingle Bells standing on the back inside the ice block. We were followed by a great, long snaking queue of cars. Everyone wanted to catch a glimpse of the cow inside the ice block.

After a couple of hours we turned off a side road and headed for the hills. There was no one following us. I hoped.

We went by streams and stretching farms. We went through gum forests and wattle-lined roads. 'This is more like it,' I said. 'This is where Jingle Bells belongs.'

At last we came to a quiet, shady glen. There was long,

cool grass surrounded by a leafy gum forest. There were no fences. 'This is it Jack,' I said. 'This is what we have been looking for.'

We drove the truck into the middle of the field and stopped. Then we unloaded Jingle Bells onto the grass. The ice had melted a fair bit. Her horns were sticking out into the air. I took a shovel out of the truck.

'What's that for?' asked Jack.

'To bury her,' I said. 'To bury her after the ice melts.'

'Don't start digging yet,' said Jack. 'Let's wait awhile.'

Jack and I sat down and gazed at poor frozen Jingle Bells standing in her ice block in the middle of the field. We were hot and tired. The bees buzzed. The birds called. The golden sun shone in the heavens. A hot north wind was blowing.

We sat and watched the still, silent ice cow for a long time. Then we both fell asleep.

I was awakened by something licking my face. I sat bolt upright. It was night time. There was no moon. 'Jack,' I yelled. 'Jack. Wake up.' I couldn't see anything. The air was still warm but the night was black.

I heard heavy footsteps crashing off into the bush.

'What is it?' said Jack. 'What's going on? Where are you?'

Suddenly the moon came out and we peered at each other in the soft light. Then we looked at the ice block. Or I should say we looked at where the ice block had been. It was gone. Melted. And Jingle Bells was gone too. Jack ran over and felt the wet grass. Then he pointed at something. It was a pat of sloppy cow dung. And footprints, no, not footprints – cow prints. Leading off into the bush.

'Let's go and find her,' I yelled.

Jack put his hand on my arm. 'No,' he said. 'Our work is done. Let's go home.'

I looked at him for a long time without saying anything. I knew he was right. I nodded slowly. We climbed into the truck. Just before the engine fired I heard something wonderful. Six, short, happy moos. They sounded a bit like the first few bars of the Christmas carol 'Jingle Bells'.

Jack and I both smiled as we drove down the road without talking. After a while I said, 'Did you know that was going to happen?'

Jack nodded. 'Well,' I went on, 'why don't you thaw out all the animals in the collection and bring them back to life?'

'Because,' said Jack slowly, 'the tank had different water. And now it's gone. I was saving it up for someone, or something special.' He wouldn't talk about it any more after that.

10

When we got back to the ice works Jack went inside the freezer to check his collection. 'Look at this,' he yelled. 'Someone has broken in.'

There was a small hole in the roof of the freezer and a short bit of rope hanging down. There was no one around though. And nothing had been touched. All of the frozen animals sat silently on their shelves.

The big bin of water was directly under the hole in the roof. I climbed up and looked in. 'There's something in there,' I said. 'And it's frozen inside the ice. Something has fallen in the water and couldn't get out. It's been frozen with the water inside the bin.'

Jack brought in his truck and tipped the bin over on its side. A giant ice block crashed out onto the floor.

We both stared and stared. Gravel was frozen inside. He must have broken in through the freezer roof looking for Jingle Bells and fallen into the water. Now he was frozen in a block of ice.

His frozen fingers were clawed as if he was just about to scratch someone. His mouth was snarled back in a silent scream. His eyes stared without seeing.

'What will we do with him?' gasped Jack.

'Well,' I said, 'Gravel starts with "G". That comes between "F" and "H". So we put him over there.'

And as far as I know he is still there. Staring out from the ice. With a frozen fox on one side and a hare on the other.

UFD

<hr>

1

You can be the judge. Am I the biggest liar in the world or do I tell the truth? There is one thing for sure – Dad believes me. Anyway, I will leave it up to you. I will tell you what happened and you can make up your own mind.

It all starts one evening about tea time. Dad is cooking the tea and Mum is watching *Sixty Minutes* on television. Suddenly there is a knock on the door. 'I'll get it,' yells my little brother Matthew. He always runs to be first to the door and first to the telephone. It really gets on my nerves the way he does this.

We hear the sound of Matthew talking to an adult. Then we hear heavy footsteps coming down the hall. Everyone looks up and stares at this man wearing a light-blue uniform. He has badges on his chest. One of them is a pair of little wings joined together. On his shoulder is a patch saying 'ROYAL AUSTRALIAN AIRFORCE'. We have never seen this man before.

'Yes?' says Dad.

'Mr Hutchins?' says the man from the airforce.

'Yes,' answers Dad.

'Mr Simon Hutchins?'

'No', says Dad pointing at me. 'That is Simon Hutchins'.

I can feel my face starting to go red. Everyone is looking at me. I think I know what this is about.

'I have come about the UFO,' says the man in the uniform.

'UFO?' say Mum and Dad together.

'Yes,' answers the bloke in the uniform. 'A Mister Simon Hutchins rang the airforce and reported a UFO.'

Dad looks at me with a fierce expression on his face. He is about to blow his top. 'This boy,' says Dad slowly, 'is the biggest liar in the world. You are wasting your time. He has not seen a UFO. He has dreamed it up. He is always making up the most fantastic stories. I am afraid you have come all this way for nothing.'

'Nevertheless,' says the man from the airforce, 'I will have to do a report. Do you mind if I talk to Simon?' Then he holds out his hand to Dad. 'My name is Wing Commander Collins.'

'Go ahead,' says Dad as he shakes Wing Commander Collins' hand. 'And after you have finished I will have a talk to Simon myself. A very long talk.' He gives me a dirty look. I know that I am in big trouble.

'What's a UFO?' butts in my little brother. Matthew

doesn't know anything about anything. He is just a little kid with a big voice.

'It's an unidentified flying object,' answers Wing Commander Collins.

'Wow,' says Matthew with his mouth hanging open. 'A flying saucer. Did you really see a flying saucer?'

'Not exactly,' I say. 'But I did see a UFO.'

Wing Commander Collins sits down at the table and starts writing in a note book. 'What time did you see it?' he asks.

I think for a bit and then I say, 'Seven o'clock this morning. I know it was seven o'clock because the boom gates on the railway line woke me up. The first train goes through at seven.'

The Wing Commander writes this down. I don't know if he believes me or not. It is true though. Those boom gates go flying up after a train has gone through. They end up pointing at the sky. When they hit the buffer they make a terrific crash. They wake me up at seven every morning.

The airforce man finishes writing and asks me his next question. 'Where did you see it?'

I point through the kitchen window. 'Out there. I was in bed and I saw it go past my window.'

'How big was it?'

'About one metre.'

He looks at me with a funny expression but he does not say anything. He just writes in his book. After a bit more writing he says, 'And what colour was it?'

'Black,' I answer.

'And what was it made of?'

'Skin,' I say. 'Skin and hair.'

At this point everyone in the room jumps to their feet and yells out, 'Skin and hair?' as if they have never heard of skin and hair before.

'Yes,' I say.

'And what shape was it?' growls the Commander.

'Dog shaped. It was dog shaped.'

'Dog shaped?' yells the whole family again. I start to feel as if I am living with a bunch of parrots. They keep repeating everything I say.

'You mean,' says the Wing Commander, 'that you saw a flying object that was shaped like a dog and covered in skin and hair?'

'No,' I answer. 'It wasn't a dog-shaped object. It was a dog-shaped dog. A real dog.'

2

The Wing Commander springs to his feet and snaps his book shut. 'Good grief,' he shouts. 'You mean I have come all this way on a Sunday night just because you looked out of the window and saw a dog?' The Wing Commander is getting mad.

'It was not just a dog,' I tell him. 'It was alive. And it was flying. It flew past the window and up over the house. It came from down there, down near the railway line.'

Everyone looks down the hill but I can tell that no one believes me.

'Did it have wings?' says Matthew.

'No,' I yell. 'Of course not.'

'Or a propeller?' says Dad in a mean voice.

'No,' I shout. Tears are starting to come into my eyes. 'It was moving its legs. Like it was swimming in the air. Real fast. It was moving its legs and yapping.'

The Wing Commander is leaving. He is charging down the hall. Before he goes he turns round and barks at Dad. 'You had better teach that boy not to tell lies. Wasting people's time with this nonsense about a flying dog.' He goes out and slams the front door behind him.

Mum and Dad and Matthew all stare at me. I can see that they don't believe a word of my story. I run to my bedroom and throw myself on the bed. I can hear Dad shouting from the kitchen. 'You are grounded for two months Simon. I am sick of these stupid lies of yours. I am going to teach you a lesson about truthfulness once and for all.'

I am sick of being called a liar.

I have tears in my eyes.

Dad comes into the bedroom and looks at me. He can see that I am not faking it. I am very upset. He starts to feel sorry for me. 'Come on Simon,' he says. 'You can't have seen a flying dog. It must have been a reflection in the window or something like that.'

'I did,' I shout at him. 'I saw an unidentified flying dog – a UFD. I'll bet you a thousand dollars that I did.'

'You haven't got a thousand dollars,' says Dad. 'In fact you haven't got any dollars at all.'

What he says is true. 'All right,' I say. 'If I prove that there is such a thing as a UFD you have to pay me a thousand dollars. If I can't prove it I will do the washing up on my own every night for three years.'

Dad thinks about this for a while, then he grins and holds out his hand. 'Okay,' he says, 'if you prove there is a UFD you get a thousand dollars. If not – three years of washing up. You have one week to prove it.' He thinks that I am going to back down and say that I didn't see the flying dog. But he is wrong.

I shake his hand slowly. I am not feeling too good though. If there is one thing I hate it is the washing up. I am sure that no more flying dogs are going to appear. I do not have the foggiest where the other one came from. Probably Mars or Venus. I wonder if there is a space ship somewhere looking for it – like in *E.T.*

3

'Come on,' says Dad. 'Let's go down and get some ice cream for everyone. We only have an hour left before the milk bar closes.'

We walk out the drive to Dad's precious new car. It is a Holden Camira. A red one with a big dent in the boot. Dad rubs his hand over the dent and looks unhappy. The dent happened a week earlier and it was not Dad's fault. The boom gates at the railway crossing dropped down in front of the car. Real quick. Dad slammed his foot on the brakes and – kerpow – a yellow Ford ran into the back of our new Camira.

'Ruddy gates,' says Dad. He is still rubbing his hand over the dent like it is a personal wound. 'Someone ought to report them to the railways. Those gates go up and down like lightning. Don't give you a chance to stop.'

Dad is especially sore because there were no witnesses to the accident. No one saw it. If Dad had a witness he might be able to make the owner of the yellow Ford pay up. Now he has to fork out for the repair bill himself.

We drive down towards the milk bar. As we get to the railway crossing I see that there is no sign of any trains. I also see that Mrs Jensen is about to cross the line with her bull terrier. This bull terrier is the worst dog in the world. She has it on a long lead. This is good. It means that the vicious animal cannot bite anyone as they walk by.

Mrs Jensen's bull terrier is called Ripper. This is a good name for the rotten thing. Once it ripped a big hole in my pants. It has also been known to rip holes in people's legs.

Ripper snarls and snaps and tries to get off the lead as Mrs Jensen walks along.

We are driving behind a big truck. The truckie is looking at Mrs Jensen's dog Ripper. He is probably glad to be nice and safe inside his cabin. Suddenly the boom gates fall down in front of the truck. The truckie hits the brakes fast. Dad doesn't hit the brakes at all. Our Camira crashes into the back of the truck with a terrible grinding noise.

Dad groans and hangs his head down on the steering wheel. 'Not again,' he says. 'Not twice in the same month.' He looks around and then suddenly thinks of something. 'Quick,' he yells. 'Don't let Mrs Jensen go. She is our witness. She saw the whole thing. Run over and get her.'

The truckie is getting out. He is a big tough guy.

'Get Mrs Jensen,' yells Dad. 'Don't let her go.'

I take a couple of steps forward. Ripper is snarling and

snapping. He recognises my leg. He wants to take another bite.

'The dog,' I say to Dad feebly. 'The dog will bite my leg.'

Dad is looking at the truckie. He really is a big bloke. 'Don't argue,' says Dad out of the corner of his mouth so that the truckie won't hear. 'Get Mrs Jensen.'

I walk over to Mrs Jensen and her savage dog. 'Dad would like to talk to you,' I say. 'But please don't bring your dog.'

Mrs Jensen is not too sure about this. She does not like me very much. In the end she slips the dog's lead over the end of one of the boom gates so that it cannot get my leg.

A train goes through the crossing and disappears along the track.

The boom gates fly up.

Ripper goes up with the boom gate. It flicks him and his lead high into the sky. Up over the trees and past the kitchen window of our house. His legs are moving like he is swimming in the air. He is yapping as he goes.

4

On the way home Dad is in a grumpy mood. He has one dent in the back of the car and another one in the front.

I am grinning my head off. I wonder how I will spend the thousand dollars.

P.S. Ripper lands in our neighbour's swimming pool. He is last seen heading for Darwin as fast as he can go.

CRACKING UP

1

Everybody gets a crabby teacher sometimes. It only stands to reason. Look at it this way: you are going to have lots of teachers in your life. One of them has to be crabby so don't worry about it.

Unless you get one like Mr Snapper.

Oh boy was he mean. He made every school day miserable. Every single one. But May the fifth was one of the worst. I remember it because it was the day we moved into a new house. This is what he did that terrible day.

1. Hit me over the knuckles with a ruler for holding the pen the wrong way.

2. Twisted my ear until it almost came off for asking Mike Dungey how you spell 'urinate'.

3. Made me say the nine times tables in front of the class when he knew I didn't know them.

4. Kept me in after school for putting chewing gum behind my ear.

5. Took me to the office for smiling (when he was telling me off). I can't help smiling. I am just a naturally smiling sort of person. Anyway, it wouldn't have hurt *him* to smile a bit. Mr Snapper had never smiled in his life. He had a mean, boy hating sort of face. You could tell what sort of mood he was in by the number of wrinkles on his face. There were so many that it took me ages to count them all. Two hundred wrinkles was a good day. Five hundred wrinkles was a bad day. They ran across his face like deep rivers of rage.

6. Forced me to write out 'It is rude to stare' one hundred times.

7. Made me take his rotten pot plant home for the night.

Snapper had two things in the grade that he liked. Lucy Watkins who was his pet and the maidenhair fern which stood in a fancy-looking pot on his desk.

Lucy Watkins was a real snob. She knew she was good looking and she knew she was smart. She was the only person in the grade that Snapper liked. He nearly smiled at her once. That's how much of a pet she was. He always picked her to take messages to other teachers. He always held up her work for everyone else to look at. And he never told her off. Even when she did the same wrong things as the rest of us.

Anyway, just before home time on the fateful day, Snapper said, 'Lucy, you can choose the person to take the maidenhair fern home for the night.' It was supposed to be a big honour to take the maidenhair fern home and water it. The silly-looking plant couldn't stay at school because of the dust raised by the cleaners when they swept up.

Lucy Watkins went out to the front and looked around slowly. She stared straight at me. I didn't want to take the maidenhair fern home. I knew something would go wrong if I did. I shook my head. 'No,' I whispered under my breath. 'Not me. Please not me.'

She gave a mean sort of a smile and pointed at me. 'Him,' she said. 'Russell Dimsey. It will look nice in his new house.'

2

Snapper didn't look too sure. He didn't trust me to look after the maidenhair fern. 'It's all right Mr Snapper,' I said. 'Give the maidenhair fern to someone else for the night. I'm not too experienced with pot plants.'

Lucy Watkins pouted.

'Dimsey,' Snapper growled at me, 'I keep my word. Lucy has picked you so that is the end of the discussion. You take the maidenhair fern home for the night.' He put his face right up to mine so that I could smell his breath (it was horrible). 'And don't let anything happen to it. If that pot plant dies I will murder you.' He drew his finger across his throat like someone using a knife. 'That pot is an antique. If anything happens to it you are dead meat.' His wrinkles were about one centimetre away from my eyeballs. I could see the hairs in his nose twitching in the breeze when he breathed.

I shuddered.

It took me ages to get home. I missed the bus because I

was kept in. And I had to carry the maidenhair fern home in my arms. It was heavy and the delicate fronds kept brushing against my nose and making me sneeze.

When I finally reached home there was someone waiting for me. It was Lucy Watkins. She was sitting on her bike with one foot on the footpath.

She smiled a mean smile. 'Seen the ghost yet?' she said.

'What?' I yelped.

'The ghost. The ghost of the boy who died in there.' She nodded at our new house.

I just looked at her. 'Someone died in our house?'

'Why do you think you got it so cheap?' she sneered. 'No one else would buy it.'

'Who died there?' I asked. I didn't like having to talk to Lucy Watkins but I had to find out.

'Well, two people actually. A boy called Samuel. He died a little before his uncle. His uncle snuffed it later. He was a magician called The Great Minto. He did tricks. And he kept things in bottles.'

'What sort of things?' I tried to stop my voice trembling.

Lucy Watkins smiled a secret sort of smile to herself. 'All sorts of things. Creepy things. Some people said he was a wizard.' The next bit was worst of all. She pointed up to the little attic window on the roof of the house. The window of my new bedroom. 'They both died in that room. And one of them is still there. On moonless nights Samuel's ghostly face looks out. An unhappy little face. The face of Samuel the sad spook.'

64

'Bulldust,' I said. 'You're making it up. You're just trying to make me scared.'

'You'll see,' said the horrible Lucy Watkins. 'Just you wait until the darkest part of the night. That's when he comes out.' She pointed to the maidenhair fern. Its lace-like fronds were gently waving in the wind. 'You had better not take it into the bedroom. You wouldn't want it to shrivel up from fright. Mr Snapper wouldn't like that.' She started laughing to herself. Cackling away like a chook. Then she rode off without another word.

3

I raced inside as fast as I could go. 'Mum,' I yelled, 'did you know that people died in my room? Two people?'

Mum didn't say anything. Not a word. I knew then that it was true. Now I knew how we could afford such a posh house. It was haunted. No one wanted to buy it so Mum got it cheap.

'I'm not sleeping up there,' I said. 'Not with a ghost hanging around.'

'There's no such thing as ghosts,' said Mum. 'It will be all right after the first night.'

'There isn't going to be any first night,' I yelled.

'Yes there is,' said Mum. 'And it's going to be tonight.'

I took the maidenhair fern up to the bedroom with me. I put it on my bedside table where it would be safe. I knew that I would have to spend the night in the room.

Mum was very strong minded. She had been like that ever since Dad left home.

I looked at the maidenhair fern. I had to admit that it was a lovely plant. Even if it did belong to Snapper. I poured a little water into the pot. I didn't want the plant dying in the night. There had already been enough deaths in this room and I didn't want any more.

It was around about midnight when I first saw Sad Samuel. I just sort of knew in my sleep that someone else was in the room. I could feel a presence. I didn't want to look but in the end I forced open my eyes and saw him. By the window. A little whispy ghost with an unhappy mouth. A boy of about my age. He just stood there looking at me sadly.

'Mum,' I screamed. 'A ghost. A ghost. He . . . I.'

The ghost didn't look the least bit surprised. He shook his head as if I had done just what he expected.

Mum crashed into the room in her dressing gown. 'What's up Russell?' she yelled. 'Did you have a nightmare?'

I pointed to the ghost.

'What?' she said.

'Him. The ghost.' I managed to gasp.

Mum peered around the room. Then she stared straight at Sad Samuel. 'I can't see anything,' she said. 'It must have been a bad dream.'

'It wasn't a dream. He's still there. Over by the window.'

Mum walked over to the window. She walked right into Sad Samuel. And when I say into him I mean *into* him. She stood inside the ghost just as if he was a cloud or the end of a rainbow. And she didn't even see him.

I felt sick. My stomach was jumping up and down. My legs were wobbling. I pointed at Sad Samuel with a shaking hand. 'You're on him,' I screamed. 'You're in him. You're standing in him.'

Mum stepped out of Samuel and came over to the bed. 'There, there,' she said stroking my hair with her hand. 'There's nothing there. It was only a bad dream. Go back to sleep. I'll leave the light on for you.'

Mum closed the door and went back to her room. Sad Samuel just stood there. I now know that you can only see ghosts if they want you to see them. He wanted me to see him. But not Mum.

4

The little ghost beckoned me with his finger. He wanted me to come to him. He drifted over to the door wiggling his finger at me as he went.

I shook my head. 'No fear,' I said in a shaking voice. 'I'm staying here.' There was no way I was going to follow a ghost. He could be heading anywhere.

He seemed upset. He beckoned me again. This time by waving his arm at me furiously. He didn't seem able to speak. Only to wave. 'You're in a dream,' I yelled. 'A nightmare. You aren't really there. I'm going back to sleep.'

I put my head on the pillow and pulled the blanket up over my head. Then I closed my eyes and told myself that there was no such things as ghosts.

The ghost got into bed with me.

No kidding. He snuck down under the covers and

started tickling the bottom of my foot with a chilly little finger.

It wasn't like getting tickled by your Mum or your Dad where they dig their fingers in until it hurts. No. This was different. It was like being tickled by a puff of smoke or the breath of a feather. I tried to brush him off but my hand couldn't find anything to grab. It just passed through him.

I gave a nervous giggle. I was scared but I couldn't help myself. It tickled something terrible. 'Stop it,' I gasped between giggles. 'Please stop it.'

He didn't.

I started to laugh. Louder and louder. I tossed and turned. The bedcovers went up and down. I laughed and lurched. I hooted and heaved. The bed shook as I shrieked with laughter. 'Don't,' I cried. 'Please don't.' But Samuel the Sad Spook had no mercy. He tickled on and on and on. The bedclothes were scattered all across the room. I bucked up and down. Laughing and giggling.

Suddenly there was a terrible crash as I bumped into the bedside table. The maidenhair pot fell on the floor and broke into a thousand pieces.

Everything stopped. My world froze.

The ghost no longer concerned me. If all it could do was tickle I didn't have much to worry about. But Snapper, he could do much worse than tickle. One look from him could give your warts the wanders. 'It's your fault,' I screamed at Samuel. 'Now look what you've done. You've broken it.' Boy, was I mad. Samuel went back to the window. Now he really looked sad. He was the most miserable ghost in the world. And I was the most miserable boy.

I couldn't mend the pot so I went down the kitchen to find something else. All I could find was an empty margarine container. I scooped up the dirt from the bedroom floor and pushed the maidenhair fern back into the container. I hoped like mad that it would live.

Sad Samuel followed me around the house while I fixed up the plant. When I had finished he started beckoning to me again. He wanted me to follow him. 'You must be joking,' I yelled. I threw my pillow at him but it just passed straight through his head. His face grew even sadder. A little, broken bracelet of tears spilled down his cheeks.

He wagged his finger at me and shook his head again. He wanted something and he wasn't going to give up until he got it. I buried my head back under the blankets and tried to go to sleep. I hoped that I would wake up in the morning and find that it had all been a terrible dream.

It wasn't. In the morning the ghost was still there. And so was the broken pot. And the dead maidenhair fern. Yes it was dead. Brown and shrivelled. Just like I was going to be when Snapper finished with me.

I took the margarine container and the dirt down the backyard and looked for another plant. I hoped that I could replace the dead maidenhair with something else. All I could find was a stalk of sweet corn. One lonely stick of maize. I pulled it out and shoved it into the margarine container. It looked like a lamp post growing out of a thimble.

The ghost joined us for breakfast. Mum couldn't see it of course. It sat sorrowfully at the end of the table and watched me eat my muesli. I didn't feel sorry for it. Not after what it had done. All I could think about was school. And a slow, lingering death.

Sad Samuel followed me to school. No one except me could see him. 'Nick off,' I yelled. 'Go away, get lost.'

Miss Stevens, the librarian was right behind me. She thought I was talking to her. 'What a rude boy,' she said. 'I will report this to Mr Snapper.'

My miserable mate followed me into school and sat down in the empty desk next to me. No one could see him except me.

'Dimsey,' growled Snapper, 'where's my maidenhair fern?'

5

I held out the sweet corn in the margarine container. Snapper's nose started to twitch. 'What's that?' he croaked.

'It's your plant,' I said weakly. My stomach was heaving around like a basketball. I felt sick.

Snapper's face resembled a wall that had just been dynamited. One second it was normal. The next it had a million cracks running across it. The wrinkles even ran up under his phoney-looking wig.

'What?' he shrieked. 'Where's my pot?'

'Broken,' I mumbled. 'The ghost broke it. It tickled me in bed.'

'Ghost,' he cried. 'Tickled.' He was spitting and spluttering. He was about to erupt.

I pointed at Sad Samuel. 'Him. He did it.'

Everyone looked at the empty seat. I was the only one who could see the sorrowful spectre. Sad Samuel looked at me gloomily. Then he got out of his seat and came towards me with outstretched hands. 'No,' I yelled. 'No. Not that. Not now.'

Snapper looked down at me with his boiling red face.

Sad Samuel's little fingers began to tickle under my armpits.

I bit my tongue. I did everything I could not to laugh. A little snort burst out. Only a little one but to me it sounded like a thousand bulls bellowing. No one knew why I was laughing.

Snapper grabbed me by my shirt front and sent me spinning across the room. 'You think it's funny do you? You, you . . .' He didn't finish the sentence. A large fish net hung beneath the classroom ceiling. It had shells and things inside it. A short length of fishing line with a hook on it hung down from one edge. I had never noticed the hook before.

The enraged teacher jumped up and down. The hook grabbed his wig and sent it swinging in the air as if it was on a piece of elastic. Snapper's bald head shone nakedly like a cracked duck's egg.

There was dead silence. Snapper glared. His icicle eyes swept the room. Anyone who so much as hinted at a smile was dead. Gone. History. Every eye looked down. Every knee trembled.

The feathery fingers of Sad Sam went to work. I choked a chuckle. I smothered a smile. I grappled with a grin. 'No,' I screamed. Then I began to laugh. Great shuddering, gasping laughs. 'Oh, ooh. Ha. Haaa. Har Har. HaaaaaaHaaaaaaa. Ahhhhhh.'

Snapper snapped. He came towards me with outstretched hands. A madman. A monster.

The laughter spread like measles. The whole grade broke up. They hooted and howled. Lucy Watkins was the only one who didn't laugh. She jumped up and grabbed at the wig. The hook caught on her sleeve. She pulled and pulled. The whole net came crashing down and buried everyone. A squirming, cackling, catch of kids.

I crawled out from under the net and nicked off. I raced out of that school as fast as I could go. The laughter followed me all the way up the street.

I couldn't believe it. I was running off from school. I had never wagged it before. I was alone (if you don't count the dejected ghost who tagged behind). I knew I was in big trouble. And all because of that miserable little ghost.

6

We trudged across the park. I couldn't go home yet. It was too early and Mum might catch me. I suddenly spied a hose pipe. I grabbed it and squirted Sam. 'Buzz off,' I yelled. 'Go and make someone else unhappy.' The water went straight through him. He just stood there with his little downturned mouth and beckoned me to follow him.

I didn't. Across the road was the cemetery. I had an idea. Maybe if I walked through there the little ghoul would disappear into a grave. It was worth a try.

We wandered among the graves for a while. You would think a ghost would smile in a graveyard but no luck. He was worse than ever. A real sad sack.

A little way off a burial was in progress. Mourners dressed in black were lowering a coffin into a grave. I walked up quietly. I didn't want to disturb them. The priest was saying a few words. 'Friends,' he said, 'this is a sad occasion for all of us.'

Cold little fingers began working away under my armpits. 'Oh no,' I groaned. 'Not again. Not here.' I fell to the ground. It was agony. It was murder. The ghost was tickling me in the middle of a burial ceremony. I rolled about laughing and screaming. Tears ran down my face. I rolled right up to the edge of the grave laughing and chuckling. The legs of the mourners surrounded me like a forest.

Suddenly it stopped. He stopped tickling. It was like a rainstorm passing as quickly as it had come. The people in black all looked down at me. They were mad. They were furious. You aren't supposed to laugh at funerals.

'The fiend,' said the priest.

'The little savage,' said someone else.

'Get him.'

'Let him have it.'

A large man grabbed me and pulled me up by my collar. I squirmed and wriggled and broke free. I ran for it. I went like the dickens. A few of the mourners came pelting after me but in the end they gave up. How embarrassing.

I puffed down the street with Sad Samuel following. Then I stopped. He was beckoning at me with his wiggling finger. 'I get it,' I said. 'You are going to keep tickling me until I come. That's it isn't it?' He nodded.

'Okay,' I told him. 'You win. Lead on. I'll follow.' I couldn't take any more of it. This little ghost was wrecking my life.

I followed him along the street. He went home and into the back shed. He pointed to a spade. 'You want me to bring the spade?' I asked. He nodded. I guessed that his feathery fingers were weak. They could tickle but they couldn't lift anything heavy.

I picked up the spade and followed the floating spirit. Through the back fence he went. Over the back fence I scrambled. Into the forest. Along a track and into a little clearing. Sad Samuel pointed to the ground in the middle of the clearing. I started to dig. After about an hour of digging my spade hit something. I pulled it out. A black, leather case.

Sam was nodding but not smiling. It seemed as if he couldn't even manage a grin. He put his fingers in his mouth and blew. At least I think that's what he did. It looked as if he was whistling. A silent spook whistle.

We sat down and waited. After a bit two more ghosts arrived. Miserable little fellows. By now I was used to sad spectres. They didn't bother me at all.

Sam pointed to the case. I opened it. Inside the lid was written:

THE
GREAT MINTO
MASTER MAGICIAN

The case was filled with cotton wool. I felt around inside the cotton wool and pulled out four small, blue bottles. Three of them had one word written on the label.

GRIN

On one.

SMILE

On the next.
And

CHUCKLE

On the next.
The last bottle had no label at all. Not a word.

7

I pulled the stopper off the first bottle. Nothing happened. Then: a whisper, a sigh, a puff of cloud. It twisted and hummed. And headed for the nearest ghost. It disappeared into his open mouth. His sorrowful face was transformed. He grinned a ghostly grin.

I opened the second bottle. A whisper, a sigh, a puff of

cloud. It twisted and hummed. And went straight to the next ghost. It went in his right ear and vanished. The look of misery left his face. The second ghost gave the biggest smile I have ever seen.

The third bottle, the one with the chuckle, was the same. As soon as I opened it: a whisper, a sign, a puff of cloud. It twisted and hummed. And sped straight into Sam's left ear. He wasn't Sad Sam any more. He chuckled silently to himself.

I looked at them for a while. They were all so happy. So glad to be dead (if you know what I mean). 'I get it,' I said at last. 'Minto The Magician somehow stole your happiness. Your smiles and grins. He put them in bottles and left you miserable. Now you've got them back.'

The three grinning ghosts nodded. I held out the last bottle. The one with no label. 'Here,' I said, 'take this as well.' They shook their heads. 'Whose is it?' I asked.

Sam put his hands together and rested his head on them like someone sleeping. 'A dead person?' I said.

He shook his head.

'A dead ghost?'

He nodded.

'Can ghosts die?' I asked.

They all nodded.

'But then you would have the ghost of a ghost.'

By this time they were not listening. They started to spin. Faster and faster. And then, like propeller blades, they became invisible. They spun themselves into nothingness. They were gone.

I never saw them again.

My feet dragged the ground as I walked home. I had got rid of Sad Sam. But there was big trouble ahead.

Tomorrow I would have to go back to school. I was really in for it.

When I reached home Mum was waiting. She looked at me for a long time without saying anything. She always did that when she wanted me to feel guilty about something. In the end she said. 'The school rang. They told me all about the things you have done. Terrible things. You needn't think that I'm going to get you out of it. You will just have to front up to the school in the morning and take your punishment. And you can go up to your room now and have no tea.'

I went up to my room. It was no good telling Mum about the ghosts. She would never believe me. I thought about running away. But in the end I decided to face the music. Face Snapper that is.

8

It was worse than I thought. The whole school was assembled. I was called to the front. Two hundred pairs of eyes stared at me. Snapper snarled. 'This boy,' he said in a loud voice, 'has disgraced us all. He ran away from school. He laughed at a funeral. He broke my antique vase. He told Miss Stevens to nick off. He talks to himself. And worst of all . . . he tells terrible lies.'

Everyone was staring at me. All the kids. All the teachers. My head swam. It wasn't fair. I was innocent. Something came over me. I don't know what. I started yelling. 'It was the ghost. The tickling ghost.' I pulled out the blue bottle and waved it around. 'His smile was stolen. Put in a bottle. I gave it back to him.'

The lines on Snapper's face united in the biggest frown the world has ever seen. His wrinkles looked like a thousand upside down horseshoes. 'Stop. Enough,' he shrieked. He snatched the bottle from my hand and threw it to the ground. It smashed into a thousand pieces.

There was a whisper, a sigh. A puff of cloud. It twisted and hummed. And headed straight up Snapper's nostrils. It had gone to the nearest miserable person.

'Your punishment . . .' he said. And then he stopped, like a startled rabbit. Something was happening to his wrinkles. They were starting to twitch. To move. Like rheumatic sticks they began to bend upwards. You could almost hear them crack. For years and years they had drooped meanly down his chin. Now they were curving upwards. His wrinkles turned to crinkles.

Snapper was smiling. The bottled smile had found a new home.

He beamed at me. 'There will be no punishment,' he said generously. 'Not for a nice boy like you.'

I went and sat down.

Mr Snapper was a terrific teacher. The best I ever had. The class even gave him a nickname.

Smiley.

GREENSLEEVES

1

My nickname was Greensleeves and I didn't like it. Not one bit. It wasn't what you think though. It had nothing to do with the way I wipe my nose. Nothing at all.

It was because of the watch.

Anyway, let me start at the beginning. You might as well know the whole story.

Dad and I lived in the caravan park in Port Niranda. We were very poor. Always short of cash. Dad used to get paid for digging out tree stumps on people's farms. He would dig a hole under a stump and then shove in a couple of sticks of gelignite. Then he would rush for cover as the whole thing went up with a mighty bang. After that he used to load up the scraps of stump that were left and sell them for firewood.

It didn't pay much. That's why I was so surprised when he gave me the watch. 'Gee thanks Dad,' I yelled. 'What a ripper. A digital watch with an alarm.'

'Try out the alarm,' said Dad with a grin. 'It plays a tune.'

I pressed a couple of buttons and set the alarm. Five minutes later, at exactly four o'clock, off it went. It played a little tinkling tune called 'Greensleeves'.

I gave Dad a hug. He really was the tops. He could easily have spent the money on himself. He was saving up for the deposit on a house so we didn't have to live in the caravan park any more. Poor old Dad. He only owned work clothes. Old boots, a woollen beanie, grubby jeans and an old battle jacket. He wasn't exactly the best-dressed man in town. But as far as I was concerned he was the best *man* in town.

'Where did you get the money?' I asked. 'You shouldn't have spent it on me Dad. You should have bought yourself a new outfit.'

'I've just landed a big job,' he said with a crooked smile. 'A real big job. We'll soon be in the money.'

2

I didn't like the way he said 'real big job.' A nasty thought was trying to find its way into my mind. 'What job?' I asked.

'The whale. I'm going to get rid of the whale.'

'Oh no,' I groaned. 'Not the whale. Not that.' I looked at him in horror. To tell the truth I felt like giving the watch back. Even if it did play 'Greensleeves'.

A whale had stranded itself on the main beach about three weeks ago. It was the biggest sperm whale ever seen. It was longer than three big houses joined together.

And just as high. Before anyone could do anything to save the poor thing it had died.

People came from everywhere to look at this whale. All the motels were full up with rubbernecks. They swarmed down on the beach taking photos. Special buses came up from Melbourne filled with tourists. No one had ever seen such a large whale before.

Then, suddenly, the tourists stopped coming. No one would even go onto the beach or anywhere near it. The whale started to go bad.

What a stink. It was terrible. When the wind blew from the south (which was just about all the time), the whole town was covered in the smell. It was unbearable. People locked themselves in their houses and shut the windows. But it was no good. The terrible fumes snuck under the doors and down the chimneys. They seeped and creeped into every crevice. There was no escape. It was revolting. It was just like living with a bucket of sick under the bed.

Sailors tried to tow the whale out to sea with a tug boat but the cable broke. The whale was too heavy.

Men from the council, dressed in gas masks, tried to move it with bulldozers. It still wouldn't budge. In the end they gave up and refused to go anywhere near it.

And now Dad had offered to take on the job. 'Five thousand dollars,' he said. 'That's what I'm getting for removing the whale. Everyone else has failed. The Mayor is desperate.'

'Five thousand dollars,' I echoed. 'That's enough for . . .'

'Yes,' interrupted Dad. 'Enough for a deposit on a house.'

I looked around our little caravan. I sure would be glad to move into a house. 'But how are you going to move it?' I asked.

'Not me,' said Dad. 'We. You are going to help.' He was grinning from ear to ear.

'Me,' I gasped. 'What can I do? Tie a rope onto one of its teeth and drag it off? There's nothing I can do.'

'You can scramble into its mouth,' said Dad, 'and get right down deep inside it. Like Jonah. Then you can shove the sticks of gelignite into its guts.'

'What,' I screamed. 'You're going to blow it up. Blow up the whale?'

'Yes,' hooted Dad. 'It'll be a cinch. No one's thought of blowing it up. The gelignite will break it up into small bits and the tide will wash them out to sea. And we will be five thousand dollars richer.'

For a minute I just stood there thinking about the whole thing. I thought about crawling into a whale's gizzards. I thought about the terrible stink. Then I thought about poor old Dad trying to save up for a house. I looked at his worn-out clothes and his faded beanie.

'Okay,' I said with a shiver. 'I'll do it.'

'Shake, Troy,' said Dad holding out his big brown hand.

I shook his hand. The deal was done. A boy's word is his word. I couldn't get out of it now.

3

The next day Dad and I headed off towards the beach in

our old truck. On the back were boxes of gelignite, fuses, ropes, axes and other tackle. As we got closer to the shore the smell became stronger and stronger. What a stink. It was revolting. Dad pulled over to the side of the road and we put on our gas masks. It was a little better with the gas masks on, but it was very hard to talk. We had to shout at each other.

When we reached the beach there were only two people to be seen. I couldn't tell who they were because they had gas masks on too.

'It's Mr Steal, the Mayor,' said Dad. 'And that boy of his.'

I smothered a groan. The Mayor's son Nick was a pain in the bum. And Nick was a good name for him too. He was always nicking things. The only trouble was you could never catch him. He was too quick. If you put your best pen on the desk at school when he was around you could kiss it goodbye. The pen would just vanish. It was no good telling the teachers. If you couldn't prove that Nick stole the pen then you couldn't complain. The teachers would just tell you off instead of him.

'We don't want anyone here while we work,' Dad said to Mr Steal. 'It's too dangerous with all this gelignite around.'

'I'm here to make sure you do a good job,' said Mr Steal. 'I'll take care of Nick. He won't get in your way.'

'Well,' said Dad, 'you both stay here with the truck. I don't want either of you getting any closer to the whale.'

I looked at the rotting whale. Its eyes were like dead white saucers. Seagulls sat on its mountainous back pecking away at the tough hide. Even with the gas mask on I could smell it. The fumes were so thick that you could almost see them.

'Now,' said Dad peering at me through his gas mask. 'You take two sticks of gelignite at a time into the mouth. Sixteen altogether. I'll drop sixteen sticks down the blow hole. For every stick you take into the whale put a match in this box.' He put a small wooden box down on the back of the truck next to Nick.

We called this the tally box. It helped us to know how many sticks of gelignite had been planted.

'If we don't put in enough,' said Dad, 'it won't blow the whale into small enough pieces. Make sure you put one match in the box for every stick of gelignite. Then we will know we have the right number.'

I nodded at Dad. His voice sounded funny inside the gas mask.

I looked up at Nick. He was staring at the tally box. I could swear that he was sneering at us. Nick was a nasty bit of work. That was for sure.

Dad put a long ladder up against the whale and climbed up onto its back. 'It's slippery,' he yelled, 'but it will be okay.' I watched him drop the first two sticks of gelignite down the whale's blow hole. Then I walked around to the whale's mouth.

My heart sank as I peered into the gaping jaws. It was like a big, wet cave. Every now and then a piece of rotting flesh would break off the roof of its mouth and fall onto its tongue with a wet thunk. I shivered. Then I walked back to the truck to get my first two sticks of gelignite.

I put two matches into the tally box and walked slowly back to the stinking carcass.

4

Dad gave me my instructions. 'Get right down inside her guts. She won't blow properly if you don't. I'd go myself but I'm too big to get right inside. You don't mind do you?'

To be honest I did mind. What if I got stuck? What if I got lost? What if the gizzards collapsed on me and I got buried alive? I stared at Dad's eyes through the gas mask and remembered our handshake. A deal is a deal. With pounding heart I walked into the soggy, wet mouth of the dead whale.

Dad went back to his ladder to finish putting the rest of the sticks down the blow hole. I was alone.

I walked carefully over the sagging, stinking tongue. With every step I sank up to my ankles. My heart was pounding with terror. I shone my torch into the black-ness and saw that the roof sloped downwards. On either side were white, glistening shelves of gristle. I forced my legs to take me forward. Soon the roof was so low that I had to go forward on my knees. My jeans were soaked with slime.

Suddenly the whole thing narrowed into a spongy tube like a sausage. I knew that I would have to lie on my stomach and wriggle in. I could hear my breath sucking and squeezing through the gas mask. The goggles were starting to mist up in the damp air. I couldn't do it. I just couldn't do it. I couldn't bury myself inside that giant sausage-shaped bit of guts.

Then I thought of poor Dad and the battered old caravan. I pushed myself forward with a great shove and slithered into the tube. I had the gelignite in one hand and the torch in the other. But I couldn't see anything. I was surrounded by gurgling blackness. I wriggled in further and further. Down, down, down into the darkest depths and all around me the dead whale's decaying dinner.

Suddenly my hand touched something solid. It was like a slimy wall. It seemed to be crawling. It was crawling. It was covered in maggots. I dropped the gelignite and shrieking and screaming pushed myself backwards. Wriggling, choking, scrambling like a fat caterpillar inside the finger of a rubber glove.

I squirted out into the mouth and slithered over the tongue and into the glaring sunshine. Then, before my heart failed me, I staggered over to the truck and grabbed four sticks of gelignite – as much as I could carry. I threw four matches into the tally box and once again entered the unspeakable jaws.

Down I went – into the grizzly gizzards. Then out. Then back down. Then out. How many times I slid down into that filthy throat I couldn't say. Each time I threw matches into the tally box but the pile never seemed to grow. I staggered in and out and in and out. My head swam. My brain pounded. At last I could do no more. I fell onto the ground next to the truck. Nothing would make me go in there again.

Dad counted the matches. 'Fourteen,' he said. 'Two more to go.'

I couldn't believe it. It seemed as if I had taken a million sticks of gelignite in there.

Dad could see that I was beat. 'Don't worry,' he said. 'You've done a great job. I'll just throw the last two sticks of gelignite into the mouth. That should be okay.' He walked over to the whale and threw the last sticks in gently. 'Right,' he yelled at Mr Steal and Nick. 'Get out of the way. We're ready to blow her up.'

Nick and Mr Steal turned to go. And as they did so, I saw Nick shove something into his shirt pocket. It was a little bundle of matches.

My heart jumped up into my throat. He had been taking matches out of the tally box. This meant I had taken too many sticks of gelignite into the whale. I had been into the innards more often than I needed to. I felt faint with fury. I wanted to run after him and strangle him with my slippery hands. But I didn't. If I told Dad he would make me go back into the whale and count the gelignite sticks. I just couldn't do it.

5

We drove the truck back down the beach to a safe spot. Everyone in the town had gathered at the foreshore to watch the big explosion. They all stood with handkerchiefs over their noses to keep out the smell.

Dad lit the long fuse that dangled out of the whale's blow hole and ran back to the truck. I wondered what difference it would make having too many sticks of gelignite inside the whale. It would probably just blow it up into smaller pieces which would make it wash away easier.

The fuse spluttered and spat. The little orange flame crept up the side of the whale and into the blow hole. I pulled back my sleeve to see what time it was.

My watch was gone. It had fallen off inside the whale.

Oh no. I couldn't bear it. My new watch. I was mixed up. Angry. Crazy. Off my head. I stood up and ran over towards the whale. 'My watch. My watch. My watch,' I yelled.

I could hear Dad's voice behind me. He was shouting and screeching. 'Come back Troy. Come back. She's about to blow.'

I didn't know what I was doing. I fell into the mouth and slithered in. Dad's strong hands grabbed my ankles and pulled me out. He dragged me back across the sand. Bumping, jerking, scraping on my stomach. My mouth and eyes filled with sand. Shells and pebbles scratched my face. Tears streamed down my cheeks.

Dad jerked me under the truck. Just in time.

Kerblam. The sky disappeared. The sun blotted out. Sand and whale gizzards filled the air with a black blizzard. It hailed whale. It blew whale. It shrieked whale. It wailed whale.

There must have been fifty sticks of gelignite inside it.

The roar almost burst our eardrums. The truck shook with the shock. Every sliver of paint was sandblasted off its body.

And when the air cleared a great lake had formed in

the crater on the beach. Not one tiny piece of whale was left on the sand.

'Whoopee,' yelled Dad. 'We've done it. We've done it.'

'That's not all you've done,' said a cold voice from behind us. It was Mayor Steal and his gloating son Nick. Mayor Steal pointed at the town.

We all turned and stared. The whole town was covered in bits of stinking whale. Pieces of whale gut hung from the lamp posts and the TV aerials. The roofs were littered with horrible bits of red and grey stuff. Windows were broken. The electricity wires were draped with strings of intestines. The streets were filled with lumps and glumps of foul flesh.

If the smell had been bad before it was worse now. It was so bad that it made your eyes water. Every house was smothered in the torn and tattered remains of the whale.

'Don't think you'll get paid for this,' said Mayor Steal in a hard voice. 'It'll take five thousand dollars to clean this mess up. I doubt that anyone in this town is ever going to speak to you again.'

'I can't understand it,' said Dad shaking his head. 'It shouldn't have gone up with such a big bang. Thirty-two sticks shouldn't have gone up like that.'

'It was him,' I screamed pointing at the grinning Nick. 'He stole the tally sticks. He took the matches out of the box. They are in his shirt pocket.'

'Don't try to blame my boy,' said the Mayor. 'Don't try to shift the blame onto an innocent bystander.'

'Search him,' said Dad. 'Look in his shirt pocket.'

'No,' said Mayor Steal.

Before Nick could move, Dad grabbed him and searched his pockets.

They were empty.

6

'He's thrown them away,' I shouted. 'He always does that after he nicks something. You can never catch him. I saw him with matches. I saw him. I did, I did, I did.' I was crying but I didn't care. I had gone down into the whale's guts for nothing. We would never get a house now. Never.

'What a low trick,' said Mayor Steal. 'First you blame Nick and now this grubby wrecker searches him. And finds nothing. I want an apology.'

Dad hung his head. Then he looked at Nick. 'Sorry,' he said. 'I shouldn't have done that.'

We turned and walked sadly home through the whale-infested town. The council workers were already out cleaning up. We both felt miserable. We had missed our chance to earn five thousand dollars. All because of that rotten Nick.

'We will never get a house now,' I said sadly. 'Not unless we win Tatts.'

'Or find a lump of ambergris,' answered Dad slowly.

'What's ambergris?' I asked.

'When a whale is sick,' said Dad, 'it sometimes makes this stuff called ambergris inside its stomach. It's worth a lot of money. But only one whale in a thousand ever has it.'

I brightened up a bit. 'What does it look like.'

'I don't know. I wouldn't have the foggiest,' said Dad looking around him at the bits of blasted whale that covered the ground.

When we got back to the caravan I could see bits of whale on the roof. One of the caravan windows was broken. I went inside and found a round, grey lump on my pillow. It was about the size of a cricket ball. It was a slippery glob of something from inside the whale. I took it outside and put it on the caravan step.

Then Dad and I went to help the council workers clean up. 'It's the least we can do,' said Dad.

As we went out of the caravan park I saw Nick staring at us from his bedroom window. He was looking at us with binoculars. I pretended not to see him.

Dad and I worked all day helping people clean up their houses. We collected the horrible guts and put it in bins. Then we took it down to the dump on the back of the truck. The people of the town didn't say much. Just about everyone liked Dad and they could see that he was trying to make up for the damage by helping with the cleaning up.

Half way through the afternoon, while we were sweeping up in the school yard, Mayor Steal pulled up in his Jaguar. He had a little grey-haired man with him. 'This is Mister Proust,' said the Mayor. 'He wants to talk to you.'

Mr Proust spoke with a high squeaky voice. He looked straight at me. 'Are you the boy who went inside the whale?' he asked.

'Yes,' I said wearily.

'Did you see anything that looks like this?' He showed me a coloured photo.

'What is it?' I asked.

'It's ambergris. It comes from inside the sperm whale. We use it to make perfume. The best perfume in the world. But now that whales can't be killed any more it is very hard to get.'

I stared at the photo of a grey slippery glob of some-thing from inside the whale. It was about the size of a cricket ball.

The little man was getting more and more excited. 'One piece that big,' he said, 'is worth ten thousand dollars. That's what I will give you for a bit that size.'

I hadn't seen anything inside the whale. It was too dark. I shook my head. That's when I remembered. 'Back at the caravan,' I yelled. 'I've got a bit back at the caravan and it looks just like that.'

We all piled into the Jaguar and Mayor Steal drove us back towards the caravan park. He seemed to want to please this little man for some reason. As we went past the Steals' house I noticed Nick in the upstairs bedroom. He was throwing something up and down in his hands. It looked like a ball.

When we reached the caravan the ball of ambergris was not on the step. 'Someone's swiped it,' said Dad. He looked downcast and beaten.

'And I know who,' I yelled. 'I saw Nick with it as we went past. It's in his bedroom.'

Mr Proust was jumping up and down excitedly and waving his cheque book around.

Mr Steal narrowed his eyes. 'You are not blaming my

son again are you?' He was hissing in a low voice. He was very angry.

Dad looked at me. 'Are you sure? Are you really sure?'

I took a deep breath. 'Yes,' I said.

'We want to search Nick's room,' said Dad. 'Troy doesn't tell lies.'

'And Nick doesn't steal,' said the Mayor.

Both men looked at each other. Finally Mayor Steal said, 'All right. I'll let you search Nick's room. But if you don't find anything you have to agree to one thing.'

'What's that?' asked Dad.

'That if you don't find the ambergris in Nick's room you both leave town tomorrow and never come back.'

Dad and I both blinked. We were thinking the same thing. We didn't want to leave town. We loved Port Niranda. All our friends lived there. My mother was buried in the cemetery there. We didn't want to leave.

There was a long silence. Then Dad said. 'Okay, we search the room, and if we don't find anything we leave Port Niranda tomorrow.' I could see that his eyes were watering.

7

We all trooped up into Nick's room. 'I didn't take nothing,' he yelled at his father. 'You can look where you like.' He was smirking. My stomach felt heavy. He didn't look the least bit worried.

Dad and I searched the room while the others stood and watched. We spent a whole hour at it. Nothing. We searched under the mattress. In the cupboards and drawers. Everywhere.

'I saw you throwing something shaped like a ball,' I said to Nick.

'I don't even have a ball,' he smirked. 'Do I Dad?'

'No,' said Mr Steal. 'And that's enough searching. There is no ball of ambergris in this room. I expect both of you to be out of town by first thing tomorrow.'

I looked at Dad. He suddenly seemed very old. 'Can't I come back to visit my wife's grave?' he asked.

Mayor Steal shook his head. 'A man's word is his word,' he replied.

Nick was grinning his rotten head off.

I looked up at the clock on the wall. Four o'clock. Time to go.

As we turned to leave I heard a soft noise. Something I had heard once before. A little tinkling tune. A very faint melody. It was 'Greensleeves'.

'There,' I yelled. 'Under the carpet.'

Dad rushed over and pulled back a rug. There was a small trapdoor. He yanked it open and pulled out the ball of ambergris. A little shining piece of watch could be seen poking out of it. It was my watch. The one I had lost in the whale. It must have got jammed in the ambergris when the whale exploded. The alarm was still set for four o'clock and it had just gone off.

Nick ran out of the room yowling. His father ran after him shouting and shaking his fist and calling Nick a thief and a liar.

Mr Proust started writing in his cheque book with a big

smile. 'Ten thousand dollars,' he said as he handed the cheque to Dad. 'And you can keep the watch as well.'

We both looked at the sticky watch with big grins on our faces. It was still playing 'Greensleeves'.

MOUSECHAP

1

'You're not taking that dung beetle with you,' said Mum.

'But Mum, Uncle Sid likes dung beetles. He won't mind.'

'Aunt Scrotch will. She doesn't even like boys. You're lucky that she lets you have a holiday there each year. You leave that dung beetle at home with me.'

'Okay,' I said. I put my dung beetle back in his matchbox and shoved it into my pocket. Aunt Scrotch would never know I had it.

The first night at Aunt Scrotch's house was terrible. There I was, lying in bed in the dark. Aunt Scrotch wouldn't let me have the light on. She was too mean to use the electricity. Inside the room it was almost black. There was just enough light to see shadows on the wall. Just enough light to nearly see the eyes that were watching me.

I didn't know what to do. If I screamed the eyes might get me and finish me off. If I lay still, hardly breathing, they might go away. The night was long. I could measure the crawling time by my silent breathing.

The eyes stared. I was sure they stared even though I couldn't see them. Something moved. Near the clock on the shelf. A rustle? A whisper? A footstep? My dry mouth screamed silently. I wanted to cry out. I wanted to say, 'Who's that?' I wanted to call out for Uncle Sid but my terrified tonsils refused to talk. Instead they trembled – trapped behind the tombstones of my teeth – quivering under the strains of a choked-off cry.

Two pin points of light. I could see them now. Moving silently. Blinking on and off. My hand crawled towards the light switch. I fumbled among the tissues. I found my watch. I clasped some coins. Everything except the switch.

Oh switch. Dear, dear, light switch where are you?

'Click.' I found it. The room blazed. I saw at once who owned the eyes. A mouse. A small, grey mouse. It peered at me without moving. It seemed unafraid. Then, to my amazement, it stood up on its hind legs and walked. It walked along the shelf on its back legs. Then it clasped its little paws together under its chin as if it was praying.

I picked up my slipper and threw it straight at the mouse. It scampered off behind the clock as the slipper thunked into the wall.

With a sigh I turned off the light and lay down in bed. I felt as if I was going nuts. Mice don't walk on two legs. And they certainly don't say their prayers. I told myself I was upset because of Uncle Sid. Aunt Scrotch said that he couldn't be disturbed. She said I wasn't allowed to see him. I had come all the way to their lonely old house for a holiday and now I couldn't see Uncle Sid. It wasn't fair.

Footsteps. Oh no, not again. This time they were real footsteps. Human footsteps in the passage outside. I climbed silently out of bed and pulled the door open a fraction. It was Aunt Scrotch creeping along the passage with a torch. Why hadn't she turned on the light? Why was she creeping? And why was every wall in the house lined with boxes of cheese? There were sausages of cheese hanging from the ceiling. There were cartons of cheese stacked in the lounge. There were cheeses in string bags. Cheeses in red wrappers. Cheeses like plum puddings. They dripped from the light fittings. They staggered across the tables.

Cheese, cheese everywhere.

2

Aunt Scrotch tiptoed down the passage to the cellar stairs. She picked up a carton of Edam cheese from the many that lined the walls and held it in both hands. She balanced the torch on top, making it roll from side to side. It sent creepy shadows flashing against the ceiling.

Aunt Scrotch vanished down the cellar steps leaving the house in darkness. I put on my thongs and crept towards the steps. With thumping heart I made my way down after her. At the bottom I peeped around the corner.

There was a door that was not there last time I had

visited. The door was locked from the outside with a large sliding bolt. It had a small window with bars in it. Aunt Scrotch tore away the cardboard from the carton and began throwing huge lumps of cheese through the bars. A loud scuffling, snuffling noise came from inside. It sounded like a hungry animal feeding at the trough.

'Pig,' said Aunt Scrotch as she turned around to come back. I flattened myself against the wall next to some boxes and held my breath. Aunt Scrotch passed by without looking in my direction. Her footsteps shuffled away upstairs to be finally silenced by the soft thud of her bedroom door. She was gone.

In the blackness the sounds of soft gobbling came from behind the locked door. I switched on the passage light and peered through the bars. I nearly fainted at the sight. It was Uncle Sid. His hair was long and wild. A tangled beard surrounded his dribbling mouth. Stains of cheese covered his torn shirt. His feet were bare. He was kneeling down on all fours and nibbling at the cheese with his mouth.

The last time I saw Uncle Sid he was strong and neat and tidy. He was one of those uncles who is always finding ten cents behind your ear. Or pulling off the end of his thumb and putting it back again before you can see how he does it. He was my favourite uncle. And now horrible Aunt Scrotch had him locked up in the cellar.

'Uncle Sid,' I croaked. 'It's me, Julian.'

He didn't even look up. Uncle Sid just kept gnawing away at his cheese.

I was frantic. What was up with him? Why didn't he

answer? Angry tears filled my eyes as I yanked at the bolt and opened the door. This time he did look up. Then he scampered over to the corner and peered at me with bright, wild eyes. Before I could open my mouth to say anything, he made a rush for the door and still on all fours, bolted out into the passage and up the stairs.

I ran after him. I couldn't believe what I was seeing. Uncle Sid was tearing at a large box. On the side was written BLUE-VEIN CHEESE. He was tearing at it with his fingers and his mouth, trying to get at the cheese inside. At last he succeeded. He pulled out the blue and white cheese and began gobbling it down.

The smell was terrible. I hate the smell of blue-vein cheese. Uncle Sid loved it though. He gnawed and nibbled for all he was worth.

After what seemed ages and ages he stopped eating. He turned up his nose and sniffed. He held up his hands under his chin like a dog begging. Then he headed up the stairs towards the house. Suddenly he froze. He began moving backwards. He was frightened of something.

It was Aunt Scrotch. Her mouth was cruel and twisted. And in her arms she held Tiger, her fat tom cat. 'Get him Tiger,' hissed Aunt Scrotch.

She put Tiger down on the floor and he crouched low, hissing and spitting. Uncle Sid was terrified. He backed down the stairs slowly, never taking his eyes from the vicious cat.

Tiger flattened himself on the floor and crept slowly forward. His tail quivered. His whiskers twitched. He crouched, ready to spring. Uncle Sid seemed to be hypnotised by the cat. I rubbed my eyes. Poor Uncle Sid was scared of a cat. My head swam. Was I going crazy? Was this some terrible dream?

Suddenly Uncle Sid turned and ran for it. On all fours. He fled back into his little prison cell. He darted in with incredible speed.

Aunt Scrotch was almost as quick. She grabbed Tiger just as he was about to pounce. Then she slammed the door closed and locked it. Uncle Sid was trapped inside again.

'You fool,' snarled Aunt Scrotch as she pulled me out from my hiding place. 'Why did you let him out?'

'He shouldn't be locked up,' I yelled. 'Why is Uncle Sid locked up?'

Her voice was like fingernails on a blackboard. 'Can't you see? Can't you guess? Your precious Uncle Sid thinks he is a mouse.'

3

I tried to take it in. I tried to make sense of it. My head swirled. It was true. Uncle Sid acted like a mouse. He sniffed the air like one. He ate cheese. He moved around on all fours. He was frightened of cats.

My poor, dear Uncle Sid thought he was a mouse.

'He should be in a hospital,' I said slowly. 'Not locked up.'

Aunt Scrotch grabbed me by the collar of my pyjamas and pulled me along to the kitchen. She dumped me in a chair. 'He's been in hospital,' she snapped. 'They can't do anything for him. Now I'm stuck with him. I have to look after him. He acts like an animal so I treat him like an animal.'

'It's cruel,' I yelled. 'You don't have to be cruel. You don't have to put cats onto him.'

'You stay away from him,' ordered Aunt Scrotch. 'Don't you go near him. He tries to escape all the time. It's hard to get him back once he is outside. And another thing. I want your help. I am looking for something. Something that is lost.'

'What is it?' I asked. I knew that whatever it was I wasn't going to help Aunt Scrotch. I was angry. I was real mad at her. She was treating Uncle Sid terribly.

'Your Uncle invented a new type of mouse trap,' said Aunt Scrotch. 'It is like a little electric fence. Whenever a mouse steps on the wire, its brain waves run along the wire into a little box. Then they run back to the mouse. The mouse sees visions of the countryside, of fresh air. Of fields. Of corn and blue sky. It runs straight off outside and never comes back. The electric fence makes the mice long for the fresh air. They can't stay in a house. The mice are never hurt by it. This mouse fence would be worth millions. Millions of dollars. But after silly Sid started thinking he was a mouse someone stole it. Or Sid hid it somewhere. Anyway, it's gone. If you find it give it to me. It is mine.'

My mean aunt got up and went to the pantry. She took down a jar of chocolate freckles and tipped them onto a plate. All she ever ate was chocolate freckles – little buttons of chocolate covered in hundreds and thousands. I could never figure out how she stayed so thin. You would think that she would get fat from eating nothing but chocolate. She ate about thirty chocolate freckles and never even offered me one.

'Go to bed,' she ordered. 'And remember. If you see that electric mouse-trap fence – give it to me.'

4

I went to bed and turned off the light. But I couldn't sleep. Little eyes were watching me. Little mouse eyes. It was the same mouse that had been watching me earlier. I just knew it was.

I switched on the light and blinked at the little grey mouse. It was in the corner of the room. And close by was a mouse trap with a piece of cheese set in it. It wasn't Uncle Sid's electric-fence type of mouse trap though. It was an ordinary one. The type that snaps down and kills the mouse by squashing it.

The mouse crept closer to the cruel trap. 'Don't,' I said. The mouse took no notice. It crept forward until it was almost touching the trap. Then it did something I still find hard to believe. It picked up a matchstick and held it in its little paws. Then it poked the cheese in the trap with the matchstick.

Crack. The spring snapped down like lightning. The mouse had set off the trap without getting hurt. It was the smartest mouse in the world.

I put one leg out of the bed onto the floor. The mouse just stood there. It didn't seem afraid. Then it started walking across the floor slowly towards the other side of my bed. It stopped every now and then and looked up at me. At last, seeing that I was following, it walked slowly under the bed.

I knelt down and peered after it. A mousey smell came out from under the bed. I could see mouse droppings on the polished wooden floor. There was something different about them though and at first I couldn't work out what it was. Then I realised. The mouse droppings were all laid out in a pattern. They spelt out a word. The mouse droppings formed the word HELP.

The little grey mouse had written a message the only way it could.

Before I had time to take this in the mouse was off again. This time it ran into a small hole in the wall and disappeared. It came out a minute or two later tugging a piece of paper in its mouth. The mouse dropped it at my feet.

I picked up the paper and looked at it. It was a bit of a page out of a diary. Uncle Sid's diary. I recognised his writing. The scrap of paper had been chewed out of the book by tiny teeth.

This is what it said:

I have just discovered that the mouse-trap electric fence is dangerous. If two creatures touch the wire at the same time their brains will swap over. Yesterday a frog and a mouse touched at the same time. The mouse hopped off and the frog scampered aw . . .

I couldn't read the rest of the page as it had been chewed off. My mind started to work overtime. I thought about Uncle Sid who thought he was a mouse. And I looked at the mouse who seemed to think he was a person. Suddenly it clicked. I knew what had happened. Uncle Sid and the mouse had touched the electric mouse fence at the same time. Their minds had swapped over.

This mouse was Uncle Sid.

5

'Don't worry Uncle,' I said to the mouse. 'We will get you back.'

But how? I didn't have the faintest idea what I could do.

The mouse scampered off into its hole once again. This time it tugged out something different. It was a piece of wire. I pulled out the wire. It was about four metres long with little posts hanging off it. There was a small black box attached to the end of it. It was the electric mouse fence.

Suddenly I knew what to do. I picked up Uncle and put him in my pocket. Then I took the electric mouse fence down to the kitchen. I crept quietly. I didn't want to wake Aunt Scrotch.

I set up the electric mouse fence. It took me quite a while to work it out but in the end I found out how it worked. The wire was stretched in a circle with little fence posts stopping it from touching the ground. Both ends were connected to the black box which had a switch on the side.

I went to turn on the fence but the mouse, Uncle Sid that is, was shaking its head. It pointed to a place where the wire sagged and touched the floor. One of the fence posts was missing. The electricity would go into the floor.

I reached into my pocket and pulled out a matchbox. I placed it under the sagging wire with a bit of bubble gum for an insulator.

Next I tore open some packets of blue-vein cheese. I tipped heaps of it inside the fence. Then I headed to the cellar. On the way I dropped small pieces of blue-vein cheese in a trail on the floor. I opened the cell door where Uncle Sid (or I should say the mouse in Uncle Sid's body) was hungrily sniffing around.

He came out on all fours. It was sad to see a man moving around like a mouse. He followed the blue-vein trail all the way to the kitchen. He ate every bit as he went.

The mouse stood next to the electric fence. It had one paw on the wire. It had the other paw on the 'ON' switch. Uncle Mouse came forward with a blue-veined mouth. He saw the cheese inside the fence. He sniffed. He shuffled forward. And touched the wire. The mouse threw the switch.

Blue sparks flew along the wire. The mouse turned electric blue. Uncle turned electric blue. They flashed and flared. They crackled like crisps. They lit up like light globes.

And then it was over. Uncle Sid stood up and smiled. The mouse fled out of the door. 'Thanks, Julian,' said Uncle Sid with a grin. 'We did it. We did it.'

He was his old self again. He had his mind back. And so did the mouse.

We looked at the electric mouse fence. 'It's danger-ous,' said Uncle Sid. 'We can never use it.'

'It's mine,' screeched another voice. 'After all I've gone through it is mine.'

It was Aunt Scrotch. Her face was screwed up like a wet shirt that had been bunched into a ball and left to dry in the corner. She lunged forward at the electric mouse fence.

That was when I noticed that my matchbox was open. 'Oh no,' I groaned.

Aunt Scrotch grabbed the wire with her hands.

She turned electric blue. She shimmered and shone. She beamed and screamed.

The wire fence flung up to the ceiling. The black box smashed to smithereens.

It was all over.

6

I went home about a week later. Uncle Sid tried to fix the electric fence but so far he has had no luck. He writes to me quite often so I know what is going on. His last letter was a bit short though. He had to leave it and rush out to find Aunt Scrotch. She had run outside again looking for more cow manure.

In my letter back I told him the little dung beetle was doing well. I still keep it in the matchbox. But at lunch time I let it out and give it as many chocolate freckles as it wants.

SPAGHETTI PIG-OUT

1

Guts Garvey was a real mean kid. He made my life miserable. I don't know why he didn't like me. I hadn't done anything to him. Not a thing.

He wouldn't let any of the other kids hang around with me. I was on my own. Anyone in the school who spoke to me was in his bad books. I wandered around the yard at lunch time like a dead leaf blown in the wind.

I tried everything. I even gave him my pocket money one week. He just bought a block of chocolate from the canteen and ate it in front of me. Without even giving me a bit. What a rat.

After school I only had one friend. My cat – Bad Smell. She was called that because now and then she would make a bad smell. Well, she couldn't help it. Everyone has their faults. She was a terrific cat. But still. A cat is not enough. You need other kids for friends too.

Even after school no one would come near me. I only

had one thing to do. Watch the television. But that wasn't much good either. There were only little kids' shows on before tea.

'I wish we had a video,' I said to Mum one night.

'We can't afford it Matthew,' said Mum. 'Anyway, you watch too much television as it is. Why don't you go and do something with a friend?'

I didn't say anything. I couldn't tell her that I didn't have any friends. And never would have as long as Guts Garvey was around. A bit later Dad came in. He had a large parcel under his arm. 'What have you got Dad?' I asked.

'It's something good,' he answered. He put the package on the lounge-room floor and I started to unwrap it. It was about the size of large cake. It was green and spongy with an opening in the front.

'What is it?' I said.

'What you've always wanted. A video player.'

I looked at it again. 'I've never seen video player like this before. It looks more like a mouldy loaf of bread with a hole in the front.'

'Where did you get it?' asked Mum in a dangerous voice. 'And how much was it?'

'I bought it off a bloke in the pub. A real bargain. Only fifty dollars.'

'Fifty dollars is cheap for a video,' I said. 'But is it a video? It doesn't look like one to me. Where are the cables?'

'He said it doesn't need cables. You just put in the video and press this.' He handed me a green thing that looked like a bar of chocolate with a couple of licorice blocks stuck on the top.

'You're joking,' I said. 'That's not a remote control.'

'How much did you have to drink?' said Mum. 'You must have been crazy to pay good money for that junk.' She went off into the kitchen. I could tell that she was in a bad mood.

'Well at least try it,' said Dad sadly. He handed me a video that he had hired down the street. It was called *Revenge of the Robots*. I pushed the video into the mushy hole and switched on the TV set. Nothing happened.

I looked at the licorice blocks on the green chocolate thing. It was worth a try. I pushed one of the black squares.

The movie started playing at once. 'It works,' I yelled. 'Good on you Dad. It works. What a ripper.'

Mum came in and smiled. 'Well what do you know,' she said. 'Who would have thought that funny-looking thing was a video set? What will they think of next?'

2

Dad went out and helped Mum get tea while I sat down and watched the movie. I tried out all the licorice-like buttons on the remote control. One was for fast forward, another was pause and another for rewind. The rewind was good. You could watch all the people doing things backwards.

I was rapt to have a video but to tell the truth the movie was a bit boring. I started to fiddle around with the handset. I pointed it at things in the room and pressed the buttons. I pretended that it was a ray gun.

'Tea time,' said Mum after a while.

'What are we having?' I yelled.

'Spaghetti,' said Mum.

I put the video on pause and went to the door. I was just about to say, 'I'm not hungry,' when I noticed something. Bad Smell was sitting staring at the TV in a funny way. I couldn't figure out what it was at first but I could see that something was wrong. She was so still. I had never seen a cat sit so still before. Her tail didn't swish. Her eyes didn't blink. She just sat there like a statue. I took off my thong and threw it over near her. She didn't move. Not one bit. Not one whisker.

'Dad,' I yelled. 'Something is wrong with Bad Smell.'

He came into the lounge and looked at the poor cat. It sat there staring up at the screen with glassy eyes. Dad waved his hand in front of her face. Nothing. Not a blink. 'She's dead,' said Dad.

'Oh no,' I cried. 'Not Bad Smell. Not her. She can't be. My only friend.' I picked her up. She stayed in the sitting-up position. I put her back on the floor. No change. She sat there stiffly. I felt for a pulse but I couldn't feel one. Her chest wasn't moving. She wasn't breathing.

'Something's not quite right,' said Dad. 'But I can't figure out what it is.'

'She shouldn't be sitting up,' I yelled. 'Dead cats don't sit up. They fall over with their legs pointed up.'

Dad picked up Bad Smell and felt all over her. 'It's no good Matthew,' he said. 'She's gone. We will bury her in the garden after tea.' He patted me on the head and went into the kitchen.

Tears came into my eyes. I hugged Bad Smell to my chest. She wasn't stiff. Dead cats should be stiff. I remembered a dead cat that I once saw on the footpath. I had picked it up by the tail and it hadn't bent. It had been like picking up a saucepan by the handle.

Bad Smell felt soft. Like a toy doll. Not stiff and hard like the cat on the footpath.

Suddenly I had an idea. I don't know what gave it to me. It just sort of popped into my head. I picked up the funny-looking remote control, pointed it at Bad Smell and pressed the FORWARD button. The cat blinked, stretched, and stood up. I pressed PAUSE again and she froze. A statue again. But this time she was standing up.

I couldn't believe it. I rubbed my eyes. The pause button was working on my cat. I pressed FORWARD a second time and off she went. Walking into the kitchen as if nothing had happened.

Dad's voice boomed out from the kitchen. 'Look. Bad Smell is alive.' He picked her up and examined her. 'She must have been in a coma. Just as well we didn't bury her.' Dad had a big smile on his face. He put Bad Smell down and shook his head. I went back to the lounge.

I hit one of the licorice-like buttons. None of them had anything written on them but by now I knew what each of them did.

Or I thought I did.

The movie started up again. I watched it for a while until a blow fly started buzzing around and annoying me. I pointed the hand set at it just for fun and pressed FAST FORWARD. The fly vanished. Or that's what seemed to happen. It was gone from sight but I could still hear it. The noise was tremendous. It was like a tiny jet fighter screaming around in the room. I saw something flash by. It whipped past me again. And again. And again. The blow fly was going so fast that I couldn't see it.

I pushed the PAUSE button and pointed it up where the noise was coming from. The fly must have gone right through the beam because it suddenly appeared out of nowhere. It hung silently in mid air. Still. Solidified. A floating, frozen fly. I pointed the hand set at it again and pressed FORWARD. The blow fly came to life at once. It buzzed around the room at its normal speed.

'Come on,' yelled Mum. 'Your tea is ready.'

I wasn't interested in tea. I wasn't interested in anything except this fantastic remote control. It seemed to be able to make animals and insects freeze or go fast forward. I looked through the kitchen door at Dad. He had already started eating. Long pieces of spaghetti dangled from his mouth. He was chewing and sucking at the same time.

Now don't get me wrong. I love Dad. I always have. He is a terrific bloke. But one thing that he used to do really bugged me. It was the way he ate spaghetti. He sort of made slurping noises and the meat sauce gathered around his lips as he sucked. It used to get on my nerves. I think that's why I did what I did. I know it's a weak excuse. I shivered. Then I pointed the control at him and hit the PAUSE button.

Dad stopped eating. He turned rock solid and just sat there with the fork half way up to his lips. His mouth was wide open. His eyes stared. The spaghetti hung from his fork like worms of concrete. He didn't blink. He didn't move. He was as stiff as a tree trunk.

Mum looked at him and laughed. 'Good one,' she said. 'You'd do anything for a laugh Arthur.'

Dad didn't move.

'Okay,' said Mum. 'That's enough. You're setting a bad example for Matthew by fooling around with your food like that.'

My frozen father never so much as moved an eyeball. Mum gave him a friendly push on the shoulder and he started to topple. Over he went. He looked just like a statue that had been pushed off its mount. Crash. He lay on the ground. His hand still half way up to his mouth. The solid spaghetti hung in the same position. Only now it stretched out sideways pointing at his toes.

Mum gave a little scream and rushed over to him. Quick as a flash I pointed the remote control at him and pressed FORWARD. The spaghetti dangled downwards. Dad sat up and rubbed his head. 'What happened?' he asked.

'You had a little turn,' said Mum in a worried voice. 'You had better go straight down to the hospital and have a check up. I'll get the car. Matthew you stay here and finish your tea. We won't be long.'

I was going to tell them about the remote control but something made me stop. I had a thought. If I told them about it they would take it off me. It was the last I would see of it for sure. If I kept it to myself I could take it to school. I could show Guts Garvey my fantastic new find. He would have to make friends with me now that I had something as good as this. Every kid in the school would want to have a go.

Dad and Mum came home after about two hours. Dad went straight to bed. The doctor had told him to have a few days rest. He said Dad had been working too hard. I took the remote control to bed with me. I didn't use it until the next day.

4

It was Saturday and I slept in. I did my morning jobs and set out to find Guts Garvey. He usually hung around the shops on Saturday with his tough mates.

The shopping centre was crowded. As I went I looked in the shop windows. In a small cafe I noticed a man and a woman having lunch. They were sitting at a table close to the window. I could see everything that they were eating. The man was having a steak and what was left of a runny egg. He had almost finished his meal.

It reminded me of Dad and the spaghetti. I took out the remote control and looked at it. I knew that it could do PAUSE, FORWARD and FAST FORWARD. There was one more button. I couldn't remember what this last button was for. I pushed it.

I wouldn't have done it on purpose. I didn't really realise that it was pointing at the man in the shop. The poor thing.

The last button was REWIND.

Straight away he began to un-eat his meal. He went backwards. He put his fork up to his mouth and started taking out the food and placing back on his plate. The runny egg came out of his mouth with bits of steak and chips. In, out, in, out, went his fork. Each time bringing a bit of food out of his mouth. He moved the mashed-up bits backwards on his plate with the knife and fork and they all formed up into solid chips, steak and eggs.

It was unbelievable. He was un-chewing his food and un-eating his meal. Before I could gather my wits his whole meal was back on the plate. He then put his clean knife and fork down on the table.

My head swirled but suddenly I knew what I had to do. I pressed FORWARD. Straight away he picked up his knife and fork and began to eat his meal for the second time. The woman sitting opposite him had pushed her fist up into her mouth. She was terrified. She didn't know what was going on. Suddenly she screamed and ran out of the cafe. The man didn't take any notice he just kept eating. He had to eat the whole meal again before he could stop.

I ran down the street feeling as guilty as sin. This thing was powerful. It could make people do things backwards.

I stopped at the corner. There, talking to his mean mate Rabbit, was Guts Garvey. This was my big chance to get into his good books. 'Look,' I said. 'Take a squizz at this.' I held out the remote control.

Guts Garvey grabbed it from my hand. 'Yuck,' he growled. 'Green chocolate. Buzz off bird brain.' He lifted up the remote control. He was going to throw it at me.

'No,' I yelled. 'It's a remote control. From a video. You press the black things.' Guts Garvey looked at me. Then he looked at the control. He didn't believe me but he pressed one of the buttons.

Rabbit was bouncing a basketball up and down on the footpath. He suddenly froze. So did the ball. Rabbit stood there on one leg and the ball floated without moving, half way between his hand and the ground. Guts Garvey's mouth dropped open. He rubbed his eyes and looked again. The statue of Rabbit was still there.

'Press FORWARD,' I said, pointing to the top button.

Guts pressed the control again and Rabbit finished bouncing the ball. I smiled. I could see that Guts was impressed. He turned and looked at me. Then he pointed the remote control straight at my face. 'No,' I screamed. 'No.'

But I was too late. Guts Garvey pressed the button. He 'paused' me. I couldn't move. I just stood there with both arms frozen up in the air. My eyes stared. They didn't move. Nothing moved. I was rock solid. Guts and Rabbit laughed. Then they ran off.

5

People gathered round. At first they laughed. A whole circle of kids and adults looking at the stupid jerk standing there like a statue. Someone waved their hand in front of my face. A girl poked me. 'He's good,' said someone. 'He's not moving a muscle.'

I tried to speak. My mouth wouldn't move. My tongue wouldn't budge. The crowd got bigger. I felt an idiot.

What a fool. Dozens of people were staring at me wondering why I was standing there posed like a picture on the wall. Then I stopped feeling stupid. I felt scared. What if I stayed like this forever? Not breathing. Not moving. Not alive, not dead. What would they do with me? Put me in the garden like a garden gnome? Stash me away in a museum? Bury me alive? It was too terrible to think about.

Suddenly I collapsed. I puddled onto the ground. Everyone laughed. I stood up and ran off as fast as I could go. As I ran I tried to figure it out. Why had I suddenly gone off pause? Then I realised what it was. I remembered my Uncle Frank's video. If you put it on pause and went away it would start up again automatically after three or four minutes. The movie would come off pause and keep going. That's what had happened to me.

I looked ahead. I could just make out two tiny figures in the distance. It was Rabbit and Guts Garvey. With my remote control. I had to get it back. The dirty rats had nicked it. I didn't care about getting in Guts Garvey's good books any more. I just wanted my controller back.

And revenge. I wanted revenge.

I ran like a mad thing after them.

It was no good. I was out of breath and they were too far away. I couldn't catch them. I looked around. Shaun Potter, a kid from school, was sitting on his horse, Star, on the other side of the road. I rushed over to him. 'Help,' I said. 'You've got to help. Guts Garvey has pinched my remote control. I've got to get it back. It's a matter of life and death.'

Shaun looked at me. He wasn't a bad sort of kid. He was one of the few people in the school who had been kind to me. He wasn't exactly a friend. He was too scared of Guts Garvey for that. But I could tell by the way he smiled and nodded at me that he liked me. I jumped from foot to foot. I was beside myself. I had to get that remote control back. Shaun hesitated for a second or two. Then he said, 'Okay, hop up.'

I put one foot in the stirrup and Shaun pulled me up behind him onto Star's back. 'They went that way,' I yelled.

Star went into a trot and then a canter. I held on for grim death. I had never been on a horse before. I bumped up and down behind Shaun. The ground seemed a long way down. I was scared but I didn't say anything. I had to catch Guts Garvey and Rabbit. We sped down the street past all the parked cars and people crossing the road.

'There they are,' I yelled. Guts and Rabbit were in a line of people waiting for a bus. Shaun slowed Star down to a walk. Guts Garvey looked up and saw us. He pulled the remote control from his pocket. 'Oh no,' I yelled. 'Not that.'

6

I don't know whether or not Star sensed danger. Anyway, he did what horses often do at such times. He lifted up his tail and let a large steaming flow of horse droppings fall onto the road. Then he took a few steps towards Guts and the line of people.

Guts pointed the remote control at us and hit the REWIND button. 'Stop,' I screamed. But it was too late. Star began to go into reverse. She walked a few steps backwards. The pile of horse droppings began to stir. It twisted and lifted. Then it flew through the air – back to where it came from.

The line of people roared. Some laughed. Some screamed. Some ran off. How embarrassing. I was filled with shame. Poor Star went into a backwards trot. Then, suddenly she froze. We all froze. Guts had hit the PAUSE button. He had turned Shaun, Star and me into statues.

While we were standing there like stiff dummies the bus pulled up. All the people in the queue piled on. They couldn't get on quickly enough. They wanted to get away from the mad boys and their even madder horse.

After four or five minutes the pause effect wore off. We were able to move. I climbed down off Star's back. 'Sorry,' I said to Shaun. 'I didn't know that was going to happen.'

Shaun stared down at me. He looked pale. 'I think I've just had a bad dream,' he said. 'In the middle of the day. I think I'd better go home.' He shook his head slowly and then trotted off.

7

'Rats,' I said to myself. Everything was going wrong. I had lost the remote control. Guts Garvey had nicked it and there was nothing I could do about it. I was too scared to go near him in case he put me into reverse again. I felt terrible. I walked home with slow, sad footsteps.

When I got home Dad was mad because the remote control had disappeared. I couldn't tell him what had happened. He would never believe it. I had to spend most of the weekend pretending to help him look for it. The video wouldn't work without the control.

On Monday it was back to school as usual. Back to wandering around with no one to talk to.

As I walked around the schoolyard my stomach rumbled. I was hungry. Very hungry. I hadn't had anything to eat since tea time on Friday night. The reason for this was simple. This was the day of The Great Spaghetti Pig Out. A competition to see who could eat the most spaghetti bolognaise in fifteen minutes.

The grand final was to be held in the school hall. The winner received a free trip to London for two and the entrance money went to charity. I had a good chance of winning. Even though I was skinny I could eat a lot when I was hungry. I had won all the heats. My record was ten bowls of spaghetti bolognaise in fifteen minutes. Maybe if I won the competition I would also win the respect of the kids. I was going to give the tickets to London to Mum and Dad. They needed a holiday badly.

I didn't see Guts Garvey until just before the competition. He kept out of my sight all day. I knew he was cooking up some scheme but I didn't know what it was.

There were four of us up on the platform. Me, two girls and Guts Garvey. The hall was packed with kids and teachers. I felt confident but nervous. I knew that I could win. I looked at Guts Garvey and saw that he was grinning his head off. Then I saw Rabbit in the front row. His pocket was bulging. Rabbit had something in his pocket and I thought I knew what it was.

They were up to no good. Guts and Rabbit had something cooked up and it wasn't spaghetti.

The plates of steaming spaghetti bolognaise were lined up in front of us. Everything was ready for the starter to say 'go'. My empty stomach was in a knot. My mind was spinning. I tried to figure out what they were up to. What if I ate five plates of spaghetti and Rabbit put me into reverse? I would un-eat it like the man in the cafe. I would go backwards and take all of the spaghetti out and put it back on the plate. My knees started to knock.

I decided to back out of the competition. I couldn't go through with it.

'Go,' yelled Mr Stepney, the school principal. It was too late. I had to go on.

I started shovelling spaghetti into my mouth. There was no time to mix in the meat sauce. I just pushed in the platefuls as they came. One, two, three. The winner would be the one to eat the most plates in fifteen minutes.

I watched Guts and the others out of the corner of my eye. I was already ahead by two bowls. In, out, in, out. Spaghetti, spaghetti, spaghetti. I was up to seven bowls, Guts had eaten only four and the two girls had managed two each. I was going to win. Mum and Dad would be pleased.

Rabbit was watching us from the front row. I noticed Guts nod to him. Rabbit took something of his pocket.

I could see that it was the remote control. He was going to put me on rewind. I was gone.

But no. Rabbit was not pointing the control at me. He pointed it at Guts. What was going on? I soon found out. Guts began eating the spaghetti at enormous speed. Just like a movie on fast forward. His fork went up and down to his mouth so quickly that you could hardly see it. He licked like lightning. He swallowed at top speed. Boy did he go. His arms whirled. The spaghetti flew. Ten, eleven, twelve bowls. Thirteen, fourteen, fifteen. He was plates ahead. I didn't have a chance to catch up to Guts the guzzling gourmet. He fed his face like a whirlwind. It was incredible. Inedible. But it really happened.

Rabbit had put Guts on FAST FORWARD so that he would eat more plates than me in the fifteen minutes. It wasn't fair. But there was nothing I could do.

The audience cheered and shouted. They thought that Guts was fantastic. No one had ever seen anything like it before. He was up to forty bowls. I had only eaten ten and the two girls six each. The siren blew. Guts was the winner. I was second.

He had eaten forty bowls. No one had ever eaten forty bowls of spaghetti before. Rabbit hit FORWARD on the control and Guts stopped eating. Everyone cheered Guts. I looked at my shoes. I felt ill and it wasn't just from eating ten plates of spaghetti. I swallowed. I had to keep it all down. That was one of the rules – you weren't allowed to be sick. If you threw up you lost the competition.

8

Guts stood up. He looked a bit funny. His face was a green colour. His stomach swelled out over his belt. He started to sway from side to side. Then he opened his mouth.

Out it came. A great tumbling, surge of spew. A tidal wave of swallowed spaghetti and meat sauce. It flowed down the table and onto the floor. A brown and white lake of sick. Guts staggered and tottered. He lurched to the edge of the stage. He opened his mouth again and let forth another avalanche. The kids in the front row screamed as the putrid waterfall splashed down. All over Rabbit.

Rabbit shrieked and sent the remote control spinning into the air. I jumped forward and grabbed it.

I shouldn't have done what I did. But I couldn't help myself. I pointed the control at Guts and the river of sick.

Then I pressed REWIND.

9

After that Guts Garvey was not very popular at school. To say the least. But I had lots of friends. And Mum and Dad had a great time in London.

And as to what happened to the remote control . . . Well. That's another story.

KNOW ALL

1

The old box lay half buried in the sand. I wish that I had
never seen it. I wish the storm hadn't uncovered it. I wish
we hadn't dug it up. But it's no good wishing. We did dig
it up and we took the old chest home. And everything
went wrong.

'I wonder what's in it?' said Dad. He was like a big kid.
He loved bringing home junk from the beach. Every day
he would climb down our cliff and walk along the sand
looking for stuff that had washed up.

I looked at the box and shivered. I just had a feeling
about it. I didn't like it. It wasn't like the other things Dad
had brought from the beach. His other finds were all
hanging off the walls and ceiling. We had empty cray
pots, old buoys, fish nets, driftwood, bottles and other
junk scattered about in every room. But this was
different. This trunk had bad vibes.

'Don't open it,' I said. 'Let's take it back.'

'Whatever for, Kate? There could be something valuable inside.'

'Like treasure,' said my brother Matthew. 'It could be full of jewels.'

'No,' I said. 'Let's take it back to the beach and leave it. There is something awful inside. I just know it.'

Matthew looked at me. 'Sometimes you're a bit of a know all Kate. You couldn't possibly know what is in that box.'

'It's old,' said Dad, 'and it's waterproof. All the joins are covered in tar. Whatever is inside might still be in good nick.' He picked up his hacksaw and began cutting away at the old rusty padlock.

I didn't want to watch. I went outside and stared out to sea. The salt mist hung heavily in the air. Off shore I could see two whales spouting in the swell.

I heard a sudden call from the kitchen. 'Got it. Got it.'

'Come and help,' yelled Matthew. 'Don't be a sad sack Kate. Come and help.'

I went back into the kitchen and saw Dad and Matthew struggling away with a lever. The lock was off but the lid was stuck and they couldn't get it open. I stood back and shook my head. I didn't want to help.

Then, slowly, with a creak and a groan it yielded. The lid began to lift. They both stared inside in silence.

'Wow,' said Matthew after a bit. 'Look at that.'

It wasn't treasure. I could tell by the way he said 'wow' that it wasn't that good.

126

2

'Well I'll be blowed,' said Dad. 'It's clothes. It's full of clothes.' He reached in and started dumping them on the floor. Soon there was a big pile of them heaped up on the carpet.

They weren't just ordinary clothes. They were old. But there was something else as well. These were special outfits. One of them was covered in stars and moons. Another consisted of a frilly dress with tights. There was a top hat and a black coat and heaps of other combinations.

Dad picked up a pair of baggy trousers. Folded up inside them was a pair of enormous shoes and a long false nose. 'Circus outfits,' said Dad. 'They are clothes from a circus.' He seemed a bit disappointed. I think that secretly he had been hoping for treasure too.

Matthew laid all of the clothes out in order on the floor. There was a knife thrower's outfit – it had a leather belt with places for the knives. There was a juggler's costume and a clown's. There was also a fortune teller's outfit and two sets of tightrope walkers' clothes. Altogether there were about fifteen different sets.

I looked at the two tightrope walkers' outfits – one was blue and one was red. They both consisted of tights and tops covered in silver stars. Matthew held the red outfit up to himself. 'This would fit me,' he said with a grin.

A shiver went down my spine. 'Don't put it on,' I told him.

'Why not?' he asked.

'I just have a feeling,' I said. 'I think that it once

belonged to someone mean. Someone awful. Someone cruel. Someone dead.'

Matthew laughed. 'Okay,' he said. 'I won't put it on. But what will we do with them all? And where did they come from?'

'From a shipwreck,' said Dad. 'I'll bet a ship with circus people in it was wrecked off the cliff. Years ago. This trunk has been buried in the sand ever since.' He gave me a big grin. 'It might not be treasure but it can still be useful. We'll put one of the outfits on the scarecrow.'

Dad pointed to the scarecrow at the bottom of our garden. Two crows and a starling were sitting on top of it. The birds actually seemed to like this old scarecrow. It had never worked. All it ever did was provide a handy seat for the crows.

'Which outfit?' said Matthew. 'Will we have a clown scarecrow or what?'

'The red tightrope walker,' answered Dad. 'Seeing Kate doesn't like that costume we will put it on the scarecrow.' Dad picked up the red tights and jacket and walked down the garden. He pulled off the old clothes and put the new ones on. It was the strangest scarecrow I had ever seen. It looked a bit like Superman. Matthew ran back inside and fetched the top hat. He banged it onto the scarecrow's head. We all laughed.

But the scarecrow didn't laugh.

'Its face seems different,' I said.

'It's still smiling like before,' said Matthew.

'I know,' I answered. 'But it isn't a nice smile any more. It seems to be leering. It seems to be leering at Dad. It doesn't like Dad. It's the clothes. The clothes don't like Dad because he's put them out here on the scarecrow.'

'Nonsense,' said Dad as we walked back to the house. 'Whoever heard of clothes not liking anything?' I turned and looked at the scarecrow. One of its hands was bunched up into a fist. It looked just as if it was threatening to punch someone. I had never noticed its hand bunched up like that before. I thought that it must have happened when Dad put the red tightrope walker's outfit on it.

Matthew fooled around with the other costumes all afternoon. He put on the clown's baggy pants and long nose. He really did look funny and Dad and I couldn't stop laughing. The pants kept falling down all the time and Matthew tripped over his own feet so many times that it's a wonder he didn't hurt himself. He made a terrific clown. Good enough to be in a circus. Which was a bit strange really because normally Matthew is serious and not very funny at all.

Next he put on the blue tightrope walker's set of clothes. He went down to the back fence and walked along the top edge. It was a high paling fence and it was a bit wobbly. Matthew held out his arms to the side like plane wings and started to walk. He was great. He walked the whole length of the fence without falling off. 'That was terrific,' I yelled. I gave him a big clap.

The scarecrow regarded us with its frozen grin.

It didn't clap.

That was when I noticed how quiet the garden was. There was no noise at all. Not a rustle. Not even a bird call. I looked around and saw the crows sitting far off in some trees. The birds were too frightened to even come into the garden.

'Those clothes have done wonders for the scarecrow,' said a voice behind us. 'The birds won't come anywhere near it.' It was Dad.

'I don't blame them,' I answered. 'I'm not going anywhere near it either,' The scarecrow seemed to have its gaze fixed on Dad. It hated him. I knew that it hated him. 'It's proud,' I said. 'And it's haughty. And it's mean.'

'And it's only a scarecrow,' added Dad. 'I don't care what it looks like as long as it keeps the birds off.'

The crows started to caw. Long, mournful cries like lost babies in the night.

3

Matthew went inside and put on the knife thrower's outfit. The whole thing was made of leather covered in little scratch marks. When Dad wasn't looking Matthew took a sharp knife out of the kitchen drawer and snuck off along the cliff. I knew that he was going to pretend to be a knife thrower in the circus.

I looked out of the window at the scarecrow. It seemed to be closer to the house than it was before. It was on the edge of the vegetable patch instead of the middle. It was grinning horribly. It was staring straight at me. I went into my bedroom and hid behind the curtain. I peeked at it through a chink so that it couldn't see my face. I felt a bit silly. Dad was right. It was only a scarecrow.

And then my heart almost stopped. The scarecrow

now stood on the edge of the lawn. It had moved forward about a metre while I was changing rooms. There was no one around outside. Dad was in the lounge watching the football on television.

'It's coming,' I screamed. 'It's coming.'

Dad rushed into the room. 'What's coming?' he asked.

'The scarecrow,' I said. 'It's coming to get us. No. It's coming to get you Dad. It hates you. Look. It's moved onto the lawn.'

Dad peered out of the window. The scarecrow was back in the middle of the vegetable patch.

'You've been watching too much television,' said Dad. 'I don't want to hear any more nonsense about that scarecrow.' A great roar erupted from the TV set. 'A goal,' said Dad. 'And I missed it because of a scarecrow.' He gave me a black look and rushed back into the lounge.

A little later, Matthew's face appeared at the window. He was holding his finger up to his lips. 'Sh,' he whispered. 'Come and watch this.'

I followed Matthew along the cliff until we were out of sight of the house. He was still dressed in the knife thrower's costume. He stopped at a large fence post on the edge of the cliff. Then he turned and walked backwards twenty steps until he was about seven metres from the post. He took out the silver kitchen knife and suddenly threw it at the post. It spun like a propellor flashing silver in the sunshine. With a dull 'thunk' it dug into the post. It quivered silently in the still sea air.

I didn't like what I was seeing. I started to understand what was happening but I had to be sure. Matthew was grinning. His grin was almost as big as the scarecrow's. 'Do it again,' I said. 'Let's see you do it again.'

'No worries,' said Matthew. 'I'm an expert. I have natural talent.' He fetched the knife and walked back another twenty paces. This time he turned his back to the post. 'Watch this,' he said. He held the knife by its blade and threw it over his shoulder. He threw the knife at the post without even looking. Once again the knife spun, glittering and humming in the air. Once again it thunked into the post, splintering the grey wood as its point found the target.

Matthew smiled. A happy, boastful smile. 'I'm a fantastic knife thrower,' he said. 'I never miss. Fancy that. I lived for fourteen years without knowing what a good knife thrower I am.'

'It's not you,' I whispered hoarsely. 'It's the clothes. You are getting strange powers from the clothes. That outfit belonged to a knife thrower in a circus. Now he is dead and you are getting his skill from the outfit.'

The smile fell from his face. 'What do you mean?' he said. I could tell that he didn't like what I was saying.

'When you had the blue tightrope walker's outfit on you could walk the fence without falling off,' I said. 'And when you wore the clown's clothes you kept acting the fool. You get the powers from the clothes.'

'Bull,' said Matthew angrily. 'You're jealous. You're a know all. You think you know everything.' He turned around and stomped off.

'It's the same with the scarecrow,' I said. 'It's got powers from the red tightrope walker's outfit. Only it's got something else as well. Something worse. It's got the evil mind of whoever owned the clothes. And it's coming to get Dad. It's moving. I saw it.'

132

Matthew looked at me in a funny way. 'You really saw it move?' he asked.

I went red. 'Well, I didn't actually see it but it did move. It was in a different place.'

Matthew turned round and stormed off. He wouldn't let me say one more thing. He went so fast that I couldn't catch up with him.

4

By the time I got home Matthew had told Dad the whole thing. Dad was cross with both of us. He told Matthew off for taking the kitchen knife but he was really mad at me. 'I don't know what's got into you,' he said. 'First you start raving on about the scarecrow coming to get us and now you're trying to make out that these clothes have strange powers. Don't be such a know all, Kate.'

Then he said something that made my blood run cold, 'I'm taking Matthew into town. He's staying with Aunty Ruth for the night. You can make the tea while I'm away.'

'You can't leave me here alone,' I yelled. I pointed out the window at the scarecrow. 'Not with him.' Dad's face grew angry. I knew that I had better not say any more. 'Okay,' I said. 'Okay. I'll see you when you get back.'

I heard the car drone off into the distance as Matthew and Dad bumped down our track to the front gate. I was alone. The sea was strangely quiet. I gazed along the bleak and empty cliffs. There was no wind and mist was rolling in from the sea. I looked around the landscape for comfort but there was not another house in sight. In the backyard the scarecrow grinned with a twisted smile. I stared at it like a mouse hypnotised by a snake. I couldn't take my eyes off it.

Its hat was cocked to one side. Its red tightrope outfit bulged over the straw stuffing. Its legs dangled, moving gently in the breeze.

What breeze?

There was no breeze.

I gave a stifled cry as it made another movement. The scarecrow's mouth opened. Its jaw just slowly fell open revealing a black hole. A horrible black hole. I screamed and ran into the lounge room. I looked out of the lounge room window. It had moved. It was dangling from its pole which now erupted from the middle of the lawn. It was much closer to the house.

My mind went numb. I was only a kid. A kid alone in a house with a live scarecrow outside. A scarecrow which was coming towards the house. I panicked. I ran to the front door and bolted it. Then I ran to the back door and turned the key. I checked all of the windows. I told myself that I was safe – but I knew that I wasn't.

The scarecrow still stood in the same position. I watched it from the window. It didn't move. It didn't seem to want to move while I was watching it. My heart beat a little slower. My brain started to work. I would stand there and not take my eyes off it. Then it couldn't move.

We stood there we two. We stood watching, staring, neither of us moving. I frowned at him and he grinned at me. An hour passed. My legs grew numb but I dared not stir. As long as I held the scarecrow in my gaze he would not move. The afternoon sky darkened and the sea mist grew thicker.

How long could I stand there? Where was Dad? What if he didn't come back until after dark? Would the scarecrow stalk the darkness, knowing that he was safe from my gaze? Would his powers increase at night? Would he care if I saw him move in the blackness of midnight?

I looked around for a weapon. I had none. None that could fight this terrible spectre. I had to do something before darkness fell. And then my glance fell upon the pile of circus clothes. I tore my eyes from them and fixed the scarecrow with my gaze. I couldn't let my eyes wander but my mind was free to roam. An idea nibbled away at the back of my mind. There was help in those clothes – I was sure of it.

5

I backed towards the pile, still keeping my eyes firmly on the scarecrow. I bent down and picked up one of the outfits. I put on one piece after another until my normal clothes were completely covered. Then I sat and stared and stared and stared.

'Now Mr Scarecrow,' I said after a long time. 'Now I know what to do.'

I tore off the outfit. I had a big job in front of me and it had to be done before dark. I gathered up all of the circus clothes and stuffed them into a plastic garbage bag. Then I rushed out to the garage and fetched a coil of rope, a short length of chain and dad's wire strainers. I also grabbed his longest fishing rod – a huge bamboo surf rod. My load was heavy, but fear gave me strength.

I headed off towards the cliff, pausing every now and

then to look behind me. I came to a fork in the track. One track led down to a small bay and the other headed off to the edge of Dead Man's Drop – a deep chasm between two high cliffs. Dad would never let Matthew or me go near Dead Man's Drop. The cliffs fell straight down to the surging waves beneath. Anyone who fell would not return.

I struggled on until I reached the edge of Dead Man's Drop. A barbed-wire cattle fence ended at the edge of the cliff. Whoever had put the last post in had been brave. It was concreted into the ground at the very edge. I put down my load and picked up the surf rod. I took off the hooks and tied a heavy sinker to the end. Then, after checking the reel, I cast the sinker towards the cliff on the other side. It arced high into the air – too high. The sinker plunged down into the savage waves below. I wound the line in as fast as I could. I knew that my first cast wouldn't work.

I tried again.

This time I did it right. The sinker curved beautifully through the air and landed on top of the cliff on the other side. I put down the rod and cut off the line. Then I tied the fishing line to one end of the long coil of rope. I tied the other end of the rope to the fence post.

I looked at the sky. It was growing dark. I looked down the empty track.

Nothing.

I took out one of the outfits and folded it up next to the post. All the other costumes I threw over the cliff into the sea. The greedy waves consumed them and the clothes soon vanished beneath the boiling water. I disconnected the fishing reel and lay the bamboo rod on top of the one remaining outfit.

Taking the short length of chain and the wire strainers with me, I ran along the edge of Dead Man's Drop. It was about a kilometre to the other side. As I ran I looked over my shoulder down the darkening track. Still nothing.

At last I reached the other side. I searched around in the stubble for my sinker. I finally saw it lying close to the edge of the cliff. I managed to retrieve it by lying on my stomach and stretching out my hand. I pulled the fishing line in and drew the rope gently after it, across the top of Dead Man's Drop. Next I tied the short chain to the end of the rope. Then I grabbed the wire strainers and stretched the rope tight against another fence post. It had to be tight. Very tight.

The sky grew dark. The clouds were now scudding across the sky and the angry waves below crashed and reached up at me with foaming claws.

Across the other side, down the darkening track, I saw a stumbling figure. It was Dad. He was running and looking over his shoulder as he went. Behind him, with its straw arms stretched to the sky, came the scarecrow. It strode with sure and savage steps. Its pole held in one crooked claw. Its mouth agape, twisted into an angry snarl.

I could see that Dad was terrified. He stumbled to the fork in the track and took a few steps down towards the bay and then, changing his mind, headed towards Dead Man's Drop as I knew he would.

With amazing speed the scarecrow circled out from the track, trapping Dad against the edge of the cliff. It raised its quivering arms against heavens and gave a terrible roar. I knew that Dad would be no match for its evil strength.

6

Dad first gazed down at the sucking sea and then he looked up. And saw me on the other side. 'Put on the clothes,' I yelled. 'Put on the blue outfit.'

I watched him examine the tightrope walker's outfit and shake his head. The snarling red scarecrow had tripped over. It let out a grizzly groan and then began crawling forward.

'Quick,' I screamed, 'put on the clothes. It's your only chance.' Dad pulled off his shoes and clothes, tearing at them like a madman. In a flash he was dressed in blue. He picked up the long bamboo fishing rod, and using it as a balancing pole, took a few steps out along the rope which I had stretched across the ravine. The sea called to him in a savage voice. The needle-sharp rocks thrust upwards from the smashing foam. Dad tottered and then, as if he had been doing it all his life, began walking across the rope. There has never been a feat like it. With firm, unfaltering steps Dad walked out to the middle of the rope. Not once did he look down. The skills of the long dead tightrope walker passed onto Dad through the suit of clothes.

By now the scarecrow was on its feet at the edge of the cliff. Its face was twisted with hate and rage. It bent down and tried to shake the rope but I had strained it too tight. It wouldn't move. The scarecrow tried to untie the knot which held the rope to the post but its straw-filled fingers could not budge it.

With an angry scream the scarecrow picked up its pole and followed Dad out onto the stretched rope. Two acrobats, the blue and the red, held onto their balancing poles and stepped firmly but precariously into the misty, evening air.

'Come on,' I yelled. 'Keep going. You can make it. I know you can.'

And he did. It seemed like a million years but at last Dad stepped onto firm ground. I threw my arms around him and gave him a big hug. 'No time for that,' he screamed. He was looking at the scarecrow, coming, coming, coming, across its road of rope.

'Quick,' yelled Dad. 'Untie the knot before it gets here.'

'No need,' I said. 'The birds will get it.'

Dad looked around at the empty sky. 'What are you talking about?' he yelled. 'I don't see any birds.'

'They will be here in a minute,' I said.

The scarecrow strode forward. I could see its horrible black hole of a mouth twisted with rage.

7

'Look,' I shouted. 'There they are.' Hundreds of birds swept low across the cliff. They flew high above the red figure of straw and then began to swoop. The scarecrow's hat was knocked from his head and it tumbled into the waiting sea. He raised his stick and began swiping at the birds like a man trying to swat flies. Faster and faster they swooped, pecking, fluttering, flapping.

And then, slowly but certainly, the creature of straw began to totter. He fell, twisting and turning in terrible loops until at last he plunged into the arms of the tearing tide beneath.

The birds vanished as quickly as they had arrived. Dad and I stood silently staring.

After a bit Dad took off the blue outfit and threw it into the sea. He stood there shivering in his underpants. 'How did you know those birds were coming?' he demanded.

'I knew,' I answered.

'And how did you know that I would take the track to the cliff and not the track to the beach?'

'I knew. I knew what would happen. I knew you would get across safely.'

'How did you know?' he said urgently. 'How did you know?'

'Back at the house,' I said. 'I put on an outfit.'

'Which one? Which outfit did you wear?'

He laughed when I told him. 'It was the fortune-teller's costume.'

A Little Bit
From the Author
Part 4

I once received a letter from a boy who said, 'How do you know what it's like to be me?' I was thrilled that he thought that. I don't know what it is like to be him of course, but I know what is like to be a kid. I remember it as if it was yesterday.

Take being frightened for instance. When I was a boy I was scared of the dark. I pretended that I wasn't but once the night came creeping into my room I got the jitters. Sometimes before jumping under the covers I would worry that there was someone underneath the bed. I was too scared to look and I just couldn't spend the night being terrified. So I got into the habit of rolling a ball under the bed. When it came out the other side I knew I was safe. One night the ball didn't come out. I spent a sleepless night, too frightened to look and too ashamed to yell out 'Mum'. In the morning I found an old pair of pyjamas under there.

This is the stuff of stories. I haven't put the ball under the bed into a yarn yet but I might one day. I will exaggerate it. What if the ball came rolling back at you? That *would* be scary.

My little sister Ruth used to be frightened too. She was

141

too scared to go down to the outside toilet at night. It was a terrible place. Spider webs. No toilet paper – just a rusty nail with newspaper hanging from it. And worst of all – no light. My father made me take Ruth down there. I had to stand outside in the dark. Often a little voice would come through the door. 'Are you still there, Paul?' I would say nothing. The voice would become louder and shriller. 'Are you still there, Paul?' Again I would say nothing. Then she would yell, 'I'm telling Dad.' That was serious, so I would answer, 'Yeah, I'm still here.'

Many years later I wrote a tale called 'Skeleton on the Dunny'† about a boy who was too frightened to go to the loo. I also wrote a book called *Grandad's Gifts*†† which tells the story of a boy who heard a noise in the cupboard at night. For the picture book, Peter Gouldthorpe painted a picture of that boy quivering under the sheets. I have it on my bedroom wall. Every night when I go to bed I think, 'That boy is me.'

I have heard millions of noises in the night. But there has never been anything there. Thank goodness.

Paul

† *'Skeleton on the Dunny' is published in* Unreal!.

†† *'Grandad's Gifts' is published in* Unbearable!.

About Paul Jennings

'The biggest sin in writing is to be boring.'
                                    Paul Jennings

Paul Jennings's amazing success story began in December 1985, when *Unreal!* was published in Australia. Within months it was on the best-seller lists and in every child's schoolbag, and there it has stayed. It's been the same story with every book ever since.

Spooky, funny, naughty, yucky, always wacky, and always with a surprise ending, Paul's stories are devoured by readers of all ages. Every year his books top the lists of nominations for the Australian state awards chosen by children. In 1992, Paul won an award in every children's choice list throughout Australia.

In 1990, a thirteen-part television series based upon Paul's early stories was screened in Australia and in the UK. *Round the Twist* received critical acclaim from both countries. The second series, screened in 1993, was the top-rated children's program in both countries. Both series have since been shown in over forty countries throughout the world. Paul wrote the screenplays, and both times he won an AWGIE (Australian Writer's Guild)

Award. The second series was also a finalist for Oustanding Achievement in Programming for Children and Young People in the 1993 International Emmy Awards.

In the United States, *Unmentionable!* was named an ALA Recommended Book for Reluctant Readers; *Unreal!* and *Uncanny!* were both Bank Street College Children's Books of the Year; and *Unreal!* was on New York Public Library's list of "100 Titles for Reading and Sharing."

More than two million copies of Paul Jennings's books have been sold throughout the world. He receives thousands of fan letters every year and replies to them all (if they include a return address).

"Jennings has found the perfect formula for the scary and supernatural sprinkled with just the right touch of hilarity . . . Don't miss out on the fun here."

School Library Journal,
starred review for Unreal!

OTHER TERRIFIC BOOKS BY PAUL JENNINGS!

☆☆☆☆☆☆☆☆☆☆☆☆☆☆☆☆☆☆☆☆☆☆☆☆☆☆☆☆

Do you loved to be surprised? Grossed out? A little bit scared? Then you'll want to get your hands on these books!

Unreal!
Eight Surprising Stories

These spooky stories will really rattle your bones!

A Bank Street Children's Book of the Year
New York Public Library '100 Titles for Reading and Sharing'
Winner of the 1987 Young Australians' Best Book Award
Winner of the 1989 West Australian Young Readers' Book Award
Winner of the 1990 Kids Own Australian Literature Award
Winner of the 1992 Kids Reading Oz Choice Award

Unbelievable!
More Surprising Stories

You'll never guess what's going to happen, because these stories are really unbelievable!

Winner of the 1988 Young Australians' Best Book Award
Winner of the 1990 Kids Reading Oz Choice Award

OTHER TERRIFIC BOOKS BY PAUL JENNINGS!
☆☆☆☆☆☆☆☆☆☆☆☆☆☆☆☆☆☆☆☆☆☆☆☆☆☆☆

Quirky Tails
More Oddball Stories

Eight hilarious (and bizarre!) stories, all of them with endings that'll make your hair stand on end.

Winner of the 1992 Young Australians' Best Book Award

Unbearable!
More Bizarre Stories

More outrageous reading that you won't want to put down!

Winner of the 1993 Young Australians' Best Book Award
Winner of the 1991 and 1993 Kids Own Australian Literature Award

OTHER TERRIFIC BOOKS BY PAUL JENNINGS!

☆☆☆☆☆☆☆☆☆☆☆☆☆☆☆☆☆☆☆☆☆☆☆☆☆☆☆☆

Unmentionable!
More Amazing Stories

Locked in the bathroom ... Kissing a cold, cold kid ... Burning your behind ... it could only be by Paul Jennings!

An ALA Recommended Book for Reluctant Readers
Winner of the 1992 Young Australians' Best Book Award
Winner of the 1992 Kids Own Australian Literature Award

Undone!
More Mad Endings

Plans come undone. Zippers come undone. Bullies come undone. And so will the readers who try to predict the endings of these stories!

Winner of the 1993 Kids Reading Oz Choice Award